THE CITADEL
OF WEEPING PEARLS

Aliette de Bodard

THE CITADEL
OF WEEPING PEARLS

Aliette de Bodard

Published by JABberwocky Literary Agency, Inc.

THE CITADEL OF WEEPING PEARLS
by Aliette de Bodard

Cover art © 2017 by Maurizio Manzieri
Cover layout by Maurizio Manzieri
Interior layout by Aliette de Bodard

Copyright © 2017 by Aliette de Bodard
Published in 2017 by JABberwocky Literary Agency, Inc., in
association with the Zeno Agency Ltd

www.awfulagent.com/ebooks

Originally published by *Asimov's*, 2015

ISBN 978-1-625672-55-1

Acknowledgements

My deepest thanks to the Villa Diodati Workshop in La Pommeraie (Grayson Bray Morris, Jeffrey Spock, Ruth Nestvold, Nancy Fulda, and Sylvia Spruck Wrigley) for slogging through the first confused opening words of this, and special thanks to Sylvia who stuck around for the rewrite. Haralambi Markov and Juliette Wade read the entire manuscript and provided very detailed and useful notes.

Thanks to John Berlyne for shopping this around, to Sheila Williams at *Asimov's* for publishing such a long and convoluted story, and to Maurizio Manzieri for giving it such great cover art. And to Rochita Loenen-Ruiz for the constant support and abiding friendship: you are my inspiration.

And to my husband Matthieu and my sons the snakelet and the librarian, for reminding me the world is ever full of wonders and grace.

The Officer

There was a sound, on the edge of sleep: Suu Nuoc wasn't sure if it was a bell and a drum calling for enlightenment; or the tactics-master sounding the call to arms; in that breathless instant—hanging like a bead of blood from a sword's blade—that marked the boundary between the stylised life of the court and the confused, lawless fury of the battlefield.

"Book of Heaven, Book of Heaven."

The soft, reedy voice echoed under the dome of the ceiling; but the room itself had changed—receding, taking on the shape of the mindship—curved metal corridors with scrolling columns of memorial excerpts, the oily sheen of the Mind's presence spread over the watercolours of starscapes and the carved longevity character at the head of the bed—for a confused, terrible moment as Suu Nuoc woke up, he wasn't sure if he was still in his bedroom in the Purple Forbidden City on the First Planet, or hanging, weightless, in the void of space.

It wasn't a dream. It was the mindship: *The Turtle's Golden Claw*, the only one addressing Suu Nuoc with that peculiar form of his title, the one that the Empress had conferred on him half out of awe, half out of jest.

The Turtle's Golden Claw wasn't there in his bedroom,

of course: she was a Mind, an artificial intelligence encased in the heartroom of a ship; and she was too heavy to leave orbit. But she was good at things; and one of them was hacking his comms, and using the communal network to project new surroundings over his bedroom.

"Ship," he whispered, the words tasting like grit on his tongue. His eyes felt glued together; his brain still fogged by sleep. "It's the Bi-Hour of the Tiger." People plotted or made love or slept the sleep of the just; they didn't wake up and found themselves dragged into an impossible conversation.

But then, of course, *The Turtle's Golden Claw* was technically part of the Imperial family: before her implantation in the ship that would become her body, the Mind had been borne by Thousand-Heart Ngoc Ha, the Empress's youngest daughter. *The Turtle's Golden Claw* was mostly sweet; but sometimes she could act with the same casual arrogance as the Empress.

"What is it this time?" Suu Nuoc asked.

The Turtle's Golden Claw's voice was thin and quivering; nothing like her usual, effortless arrogance. "She's not answering. I called her again and again, but she's not answering."

Ten thousand words bloomed into Suu Nuoc's mind; were sorted out as ruthlessly as he'd once sorted out battalions. "Who?" he said.

"Grandmother."

There were two people whom the mindship thought of as Grandmother; but if the Keeper of the Peace Empress had been dead, Suu Nuoc's quarters would have been in effervescence, the night servants barely containing their impatience at their master's lack of knowledge. "The Grand Master of Design Harmony?"

The lights flickered around him; the characters oozed like squeezed wounds. "She's not answering," the ship said, again; sounding more and more like the child she was with every passing moment. "She was here; and then she... faded away on the comms."

Suu Nuoc put out a command for the system to get in touch with Grand Master of Design Harmony Bach Cuc—wondering if that would work, with the shipmind hacked into his comms. But no; the progress of the call appeared overlaid on the bottom half of his field of vision, same as normal; except, of course, that no one picked up. Bach Cuc's last known location, according to the communal network, was in her laboratory near the Spire of Literary Eminence—where the radio comms towards *The Turtle's Golden Claw* would be clearest and most economical.

"Did you hack the rest of my comms?" he asked—even as he got up, pulling up clothes from his autumn chest, unfolding and discarding uniforms that seemed too formal; until he found his python tunic.

"You know I didn't." *The Turtle's Golden* Claw's voice was stiff.

"Had to ask," Suu Nuoc said. He pulled the tunic over his shoulders, stared at himself in the mirror by the four seasons chests: pale and dishevelled, his hair hastily pulled back into a topknot—but the tunic was embroidered with pythons, a mark of the Empress's special favour, bestowed on him after the battle at Four Stations: a clear message, for those who affected not to know who he was, that this jumped-up, uncouth soldier wielded authority by special dispensation.

The call was still ringing in the emptiness; he cut it with a wave of his hands. There was a clear, present problem; and in such situations he knew exactly what to do.

"Let's go," he said.

***

Grand Master Bach Cuc's laboratory was spread around a courtyard: at this late hour, only the ambient lights were on, throwing shadows on the pavement—bringing to mind the old colonist superstitions of fox shapeshifters and blood-sucking demons.

It was the dry season in the Forbidden Purple City, and Bach Cuc had set up installations on trestle tables in the courtyard—Suu Nuoc didn't remember what half the assemblages of wires and metal were, and didn't much care.

"Where was she when you saw her last?" he asked *The Turtle's Golden Claw.*

The ship couldn't descend from orbit around the First Planet, of course; she'd simply animated an avatar of herself. Most mindships chose something the size of a child or a Mind; *The Turtle's Golden* Claw's avatar was as small as a clenched fist, but perfect, rendering in exquisite detail the contours of her hull, the protrusions of her thrusters—if Suu Nuoc had been inclined to squint, he was sure he'd have caught a glimpse of the orchids painted near the prow.

"Inside," *The Turtle's Golden Claw* said. "Tinkering with things." She sounded like she'd recovered; her voice was cool again, effortlessly taking on the accents and vocabulary of the court. She made Suu Nuoc feel like a fish out of water; but at least he wouldn't have to deal with a panicked, bewildered mindship—he was no mother, no master of wind and water, and would have had no idea how to do in this situation.

He followed the ship into one of the largest pavilions: the outside was lacquered wood, painstakingly recreated identical to Old Earth design, with thin metal tiles embossed with longevity symbols. The inside, however, was more modern, a mess of tables with instruments: the communal network a knot of virtual messages with cryptic reminders like "put more khi at G4" and "redo the connections, please", notes left by researchers to themselves and to each other.

He kept a wary eye on the room—two tables, loaded with instruments; a terminal, blinking forlornly in a corner; a faint smell he couldn't quite identify on the air: charred wood, with a tinge of a sharper, sweeter flavour, as if someone had burnt lime or longan fruit. No threat that he could see; but equally, a slow, spreading silence characteristic of hastily emptied room.

"Is anyone here?" Suu Nuoc asked—superfluous, really. The network would have told him if there were, but he was too used to battlefields, where one could not afford to rely on its presence or its integrity.

"She's not here," *The Turtle's Golden Claw* said, slowly,

patiently; an adult to a child. As if he needed another patronising highborn of the court... But she was his charge; and so, technically, was Grand Master Bach Cuc, the Citadel project being under the watchful eye of the military. Even if he understood next to nothing about the science.

"I can see that." Suu Nuoc's eye was caught by the door at the furthest end of the room: the access to the shielded chamber, gaping wide open, the harmonisation arch showing up as de-activated on his network access. No one inside, then.

Except... he walked up to it and peered inside, careful to remain on the right side of the threshold. Harmonisation arches decontaminated, made sure the environment on the other side was sterile; and the cleansing of extraneous particles from every pore of his skin was an unpleasant process he would avoid if he could. There was nothing; and no one; no virtual notes or messages, just helpful prompts from the communal network, offering to tell him what the various machines in the chamber did—pointing him to Grand Master Bach Cuc's progress reports.

Not what he was interested in, currently.

He had another look around the room. *The Turtle's Golden Claw* had said Grand Master Bach Cuc had vanished mid-call. But there was nothing here that suggested anything beyond a normal night, the laboratory deserted because the researchers had gone to bed.

Except...

His gaze caught on the table by the harmonisation arch. There was an object there, but he couldn't tell what it was because Grand Master Bach Cuc had laid her seal on it, hiding it from the view of anyone who didn't have the proper access privileges—a private seal, one that wouldn't vanish even if the communal network was muted. Suu Nuoc walked towards it, hesitating. So far, he had done Bach Cuc the courtesy of not using his accesses as an Official of the First Rank; hadn't broken into her private notes or correspondences, as he would have been entitled to. Long Quan would have called him weak—behind his back when he wasn't listening, of course, his aide wasn't that foolish—but he knew better than to use his accesses unwisely. There were those at the court that hadn't forgiven him for rising so high, so quickly; without years of learning the classics to pass the examinations, years of toiling in some less prestigious job in the College of Brushes until the court recognised his merit. They called him the Empress's folly—never mind his successes as a general, the battle of Four Stations, the crushing of the rebel army at He Huong, the successful invasion of the Smoke People's territory: all they remembered was that he had once slept with the Empress, and been elevated to a rank far exceeding what was proper for a former (or current) favourite.

But *The Turtle's Golden Claw* wasn't flighty, or likely to panic over nothing. Suu Nuoc reached out, invoking his privileged access—the seal wavered and disappeared. Beneath it was...

He sucked in a deep breath—clarity filling his mind like a pane of ice, everything in the room sharpened to unbearable focus; the harmonisation arch limned with cold, crystalline light, as cutting as the edges of a scalpel.

The seal had hidden five pellets of metal; dropped casually into a porcelain bowl like discarded food, and still smelling, faintly, of anaesthetic and disinfectant.

Mem-Implants. Ancestor implants. The link between the living and the memories of their ancestors: the repository of ghost-personalities who would dispense advice and knowledge on everything from navigating court intrigues to providing suitable responses in discussions replete with literary allusions. Five of them; no wonder Grand Master Bach Cuc had always been so graceful, so effortless at showing the proper levels of address and languages whatever the situation.

To so casually discard such precious allies—no, you didn't leave those behind, not for any reason.

But why would an abductor leave these behind?

"She wouldn't remove—" *The Turtle's Golden Claw* said. Suu Nuoc lifted a hand to interrupt the obvious.

"I need to know where the Grand Master's research stood. Concisely." There wasn't much time, and evidence was vanishing as they spoke. The ship would know that, too.

The Turtle's Golden Claw didn't make the mocking comment he'd expected—the one about Suu Nuoc being Supervisor of Military Research and barely enough mathematics to operate an abacus. "You can access the logs of my last journeys into deep spaces," she said, slowly. "I brought back samples for her."

Travel logs. Suu Nuoc asked his own, ordinary implants to compile every note in the room by owner and chronological order.

"Did Grand Master Bach Cuc know where the Citadel was?" he asked. That was, after all, what those travels were meant to achieve: *The Turtle's Golden Claw*, Bach Cuc's masterpiece, diving into the furthest deep spaces, seeking traces of something that had vanished many years ago, in a time when Suu Nuoc was still a dream in his parents' minds.

The Citadel of Weeping Pearls—and, with it, its founder and ruler, the Empress's eldest and favourite daughter, Bright Princess Ngoc Minh.

The Citadel had been Ngoc Minh's refuge, her domain away from the court after her last, disastrous quarrel with her mother and her flight from the First Planet. Until the Empress, weary of her daughter's defiance, had sent the Imperial Armies to destroy it—and the Citadel vanished in a single night with all souls onboard, never to reappear.

"There were... trace elements from orbitals and ships," *The Turtle's Golden Claw* said, slowly, cautiously; he had the feeling she was translating into a language he could understand—was it mindship stuff, or merely scientific language? "Images and memories of dresses; and porcelain dishes..." The ship paused, hovering before the harmonisation arch. "Everything as fresh as if they'd been made yesterday."

"I understood that much," Suu Nuoc said, wryly. He didn't know what arguments Grand Master Bach Cuc had used to sway the Empress; but Bach Cuc's theory about deep spaces was well known—about the furthest corners, where time flowed at different rate and folded back onto itself, so that the past was but a handspan away—so that the Citadel, which had vanished without a trace thirty years ago, could be found in the vastness of space.

If you were a mindship, of course; humans couldn't go in that deep and hope to survive.

"Then you'll understand why she was excited," *The Turtle's Golden Claw* said.

"Yes." He could imagine it—Grand Master Bach Cuc would have been cautious, the ship ecstatic. "She thought you were close."

"No," *The Turtle's Golden Claw* said. "You don't understand, Book of Heaven. There were a few analyses to run before she could pinpoint a—a location I could latch on. But she thought she had the trail. That I could plunge back into deep spaces, and follow it to wherever the Citadel was hiding itself. She thought she could find Bright Princess Ngoc Minh and her people."

Suu Nuoc was silent, then, staring at the harmonisation arch.

He wasn't privy to the thoughts of the Empress anymore; he didn't know why she wanted Bright Princess Ngoc Minh back.

Some said she was getting soft, and regretted quarrelling with her daughter. Some said she wanted the weapons that Bright Princess Ngoc Minh had designed, the technologies that had enabled the citadel to effortlessly evade every Outsider or Dai Viet battalion sent to apprehend her. And still others thought that the Empress's long life was finally running to an end, and that she wanted Ngoc Minh to be her heir, over the dozen daughters and sons within the Purple Forbidden City.

Suu Nuoc had heard all of those rumours. In truth, he didn't much care: the Empress's will was absolute, and it wasn't his place to question it. But he had listened in enough shuttles and pavilions; and his spies had reported enough gossip from poetry club competitions and celebratory banquets, to know that not everyone welcomed the prospect of the princess's return.

Bright Princess Ngoc Minh had been blunt, and unpleasant; and many had not forgiven her for disregarding her mother's orders and marrying a minor station-born; and still others didn't much care about her, but thought she would disrupt court life—and thus threaten the privileges they'd gained from attending one or another of the princes and princesses. One was not meant, of course, to gainsay the Empress's orders; but there were other ways to disobey...

"Book of Heaven?"

Suu Nuoc swallowed past the bile in his throat. "We must report this to the Empress. Now."

The Engineer

Diem Huong had been six when the Citadel of Weeping Pearls had vanished. Her last, and most vivid memory of it was of standing on the decks of one of the ships—Attained Serenity, or perhaps Pine Ermitage—gazing out at the stars. Mother held her hand; around them, various inhabitants flickered in and out of existence, teleporting from one to another of the ships that made up the city. Everything was bathed in the same cold, crisp air of the Citadel—a feeling that invigorated the bones and sharpened the breath in one's lungs until it could have cut through diamonds.

"It still stands," Mother said, to her neighbour: a tall, corpulent man dressed in robes of indigo, embroidered with cranes in flight. "The Bright Princess will protect us, to the end. I have faith..."

Diem Huong was trying to see the stars better—standing on tiptoe with her arms leaning on the bay window, twisting so that the ships of the Citadel moved out of her way. Thuy had told her that, if you could line things up right, you had a view all the way to the black hole near the Thirtieth Planet. A real black hole—she kind of hoped she'd see ships sucked into it, though Thuy had always been a liar.

The man said something Diem Huong didn't remember; Mother answered something equally unintelligible, though she sounded worried. Then she caught sight of what Diem Huong was doing. "Child, no! Don't shame me by behaving like a little savage."

It had been thirty years, and she didn't know—not anymore—which parts of it were true, and which parts she had embellished. Had she only imagined the worry in Mother's voice? Certainly there had been no worry when she and Father had boarded the ship back to the Scattered Pearls orbitals—enjoy your holiday, Mother had said, smiling and hugging them as if nothing were wrong. I will join you soon.

But she never had.

On the following morning, as they docked into the Central orbital of the Scattered Pearls, the news came via mindship: that the Citadel had vanished in a single night with all its citizens, and was nowhere to be found. The Empire's invading army—the soldiers tasked by the Empress to burn the Citadel to cinders—had reached the designated coordinates, and found nothing but the void between the stars.

Not a trace of anyone aboard—not Mother, not the Bright Princess, not the hermits—everyone gone as though they had never existed.

As time went on, and the hopes of finding the Citadel dwindled, the memory wavered and faded; but in Diem

13

Huong's dreams, the scene went on. In her confused, fearful dreams, she knew every word of the conversation Mother had had; and every single conversation she had ever listened to—playing with her doll Em Be Be on the floor while Mother cooked in her compartment, with the smell of garlic and fish sauce rising all around them, an anchor to the childhood she had lost. In her dreams, she knew why Mother had chosen to abandon them.

But then she would wake up, her heart in her throat, and remember that she was still alone. That Father was never there; drowning his sorrows in his work aboard a merchant ship, coming home from months-long missions stupefied on fatigue, sorghum liquor, and Heaven knew what illegal drugs. That she had no brother or sister; and that even her aunts would not understand how crushingly alone and frightened she was, in the darkness of her cradle bed, with no kind words to banish the nightmares.

After a while, she started adding her own offerings to the ancestral altar, below the hologram of Mother, that treacherous image that would never change, never age; her tacit admission that Mother might not be dead, but that she was as lost to them as if she had been.

But that didn't matter, because she had another way to find the answers she needed.

Thirty years after the Citadel disappeared, Diem Huong woke up with the absolute knowledge that today was the day—and that, whatever she did, the trajectory of her life would be irrevocably altered. This time, it would work: after Heaven knew how many setbacks and broken parts. She wasn't sure where that certainty came from—certainly not from her trust in a prototype made by a handful of half-baked engineers and a disorganised genius scientist in their spare time—but it was within her, cold and unshakeable. Perhaps it was merely her conviction that she would succeed: that the machine would work, sending her where she needed to be. *When* she needed to be.

She did her morning exercises, flowing from one Piece of Brocade to the next, effortlessly—focusing on her breath, inhaling, exhaling as her body moved through Separating Heaven and Earth to Wise Owl Gazing Backwards; and finally settling on her toes after the last exercises, with the familiar, energised feeling of sweat on her body.

They didn't have a lab, of course. They were just private citizens with a hobby, and all they'd managed to get hold of on the overcrowded orbital was a deserted teahouse, cluttered with unused tables and decorative scrolls. Lam, always practical, had used some of the celadon drinking cups to hold samples; and the porcelain dishes with painted figures had turned out to withstand heat and acid quite nicely.

The teahouse was deserted: not a surprise, as most of the others were late risers. In the oven—repurposed from the kitchen—she found the last of the machine's pieces, the ceramic completely hardened, the bots scuttling onto the surface to check it withdrew as she reached for it. The etching of circuits was perfect, a silvery network as intricate as woven silk.

Diem Huong turned, for a moment, to look at the machine.

It wasn't much to look at: a rectangular, man-sized frame propped with four protruding metal struts, reminiscent of a high-caste palanquin with its all-but-obsolete bearers. They had used tables and chairs to get the materials; and some of the carvings could still be seen around the frame.

It had a roof, but no walls; mostly for structural reasons: all that mattered was the frame—the rods, cooled below freezing temperature, served as anchors for the generated fields. A lot of it was beyond her: she was a bots-handler, a maker and engraver of circuits on metal and ceramic, but she wasn't the one to design or master the machine. That was Lam—the only scientist among them, the holder of an Imperial degree from the prestigious College of Brushes, equally at ease with the Classics of Mathematics as she was with the Classics of Literature. Lam had been set for a grand career, before she gave it all up and came home to take care of her sick father—to a small, insignificant station on the edge of nowhere where science was just another way to fix failing appliances.

The machine, naturally, had been a welcome challenge to her. Lam had pored over articles from everywhere in the Empire; used her old networks of scientists in post in various branches of the Imperial Administration, from those designing war mindships to the ones on far-flung planets, tinkering with bots to help the local magistrate with the rice harvest. And, somehow, between all their late-night sessions with too much rice wine and fried soft crabs, between all their early-morning rushes with noodle soup heavy and warm in their bellies, they had built this.

Diem Huong's fingers closed on the piece. Like the previous one, it was smooth: the etchings barely perceptible, the surface cold. Would it be unlike the previous one, and hold the charge?

She knelt by the machine's side, finding by memory and touch the empty slot, and gently slid the piece into its rack. She could have relied on the bots to do it—and they would have been more accurate than her, to a fraction of measure—but some things shouldn't be left to bots.

Then she withdrew, connected to the room's network, and switched the machine on.

A warm red light like the lanterns of New Year's Eve filled the room as the machine started its warm-up cycle. She should have waited, she knew—for Lam and the others, so they could see what they had laboured for—it wasn't fair to them, to start things without their knowledge. But she needed to check whether the piece worked—after all, no point in making a ceremony of it if the piece snapped like the previous one, or if something else went wrong— as it had done, countless times before.

Put like that, it almost sounded reasonable. But, in her heart of hearts, Diem Huong knew this wasn't about tests, or being sure. It was simply that she had to see the machine work; to be sure that her vision would come to fruition.

The others wouldn't have understood: to them, the

Citadel of Weeping Pearls was an object of curiosity, the machine a technical challenge that relieved the crushing boredom of mining the asteroid fields. To Diem Huong, it was her only path to salvation.

Mother had gone on ahead, Ancestors only knew where. So there was no way forward. But, somewhere in the starlit hours of the past—somewhere in the days when the Citadel still existed, and Bright Princess Ngoc Minh's quarrel with the Empress was still fresh and raw—Mother was still alive.

There was a way *back*.

The temperature in the room plummeted. Ice formed on the rods, became slick and iridescent, covered with a sheen like oil—and a feel like that of deep spaces permeated the room, a growing feeling of wrongness, of pressures in odd places the body wasn't meant to have. The air within the box seemed to change—nothing obvious, but it shimmered and danced as if in a heat-wave, and the harmonisation arch slowly revved up to full capacity, its edges becoming a hard blue.

"Up early?"

Lam. Here? Startled, Diem Huong turned around, and saw her friend leaning against the door, with a sarcastic smile.

"I was—" she said.

Lam shook her head. Her smile faded; became something else—sadness and understanding, mingled in a way that made Diem Huong want to curl up in a ball. "You don't need to explain."

But she did. "I have to—"

"Of course you do." Lam's voice was soft. She walked into the laboratory; stopped, looking at the machine with a critical frown. "Mmm."

"It's not working?" Diem Huong asked, her heart in her throat.

"I don't know," Lam said. "Let me remind you no one's tried this before."

"I thought that was the point. You said everyone was wrong."

"Not in so many words, no." Lam knelt by the rods, started to reach out a hand; and changed her mind. "I merely said some approaches had no chance of working. It has to do with the nature of deep spaces."

"The mindships' deep spaces?"

"They don't belong to the mindships," Lam said, absent-mindedly—the role of teacher came to her naturally, and after all, who was Diem Huong to blame her? Lam had built all of this; she deserved a little showing off. "The ships merely... cross them to get elsewhere? Space gets weird within deep spaces, that's why you get to places earlier than you should be allowed to. And where space gets weird, time gets weird too."

She called up a control screen: out of deference to Diem Huong, she displayed it rather than merely keeping it on her implants. Her hand moved in an ever-quickening dance, sliding one cursor after the other, moving one dial after the next—a ballet of shifting colours and displays that she seemed to navigate as fast as she breathed, as utterly focused and at ease as Diem Huong was with her morning exercises.

Then she paused; and left the screen hanging in the air, filled with the red of New Year's lanterns. "Heaven help me. I think it's working."

Working. Emperor in Heaven, it was working. Lam's words—she knew what she was talking about—made it all real. "You think—" She hardly dared to imagine. She would see the Citadel of Weeping Pearls again—would talk to Mother again, know why she and Father had been abandoned...

Lam walked closer to the harmonisation arch, frowning. Without warning, she uncoiled, as fluid as a fighter, and threw something she held in her hand. It passed through the door—a small, elongated shape like a pebble—arched on its descent downwards; and faded as it did so, until a translucent shadow settled on the floor—and dwindled away to nothing.

On the display screen, a cursor slid all the way to the left. Diem Huong looked at Lam, questioningly. "It's gone back? In time?"

Lam peered at the display, and frowned again. "Looks like it. I entered the time you gave me, about ten days before the Citadel vanished. " She didn't sound convinced. Diem Huong didn't blame her. It was a mad, unrealistic adventure—but then, the Citadel had been a mad adventure in the first place, in so many ways, a rebellion of Bright Princess Ngoc Minh and her followers against the staidness of court life.

A mad, unrealistic adventure—until it had vanished.

Lam walked back to the display. Slowly, gently, she slid the cursor back to the right. At first, Diem Huong thought nothing had happened; but then, gradually, she saw a shadow; and then a translucent mass; and then the inkstone that Lam had thrown became visible again on the floor of the machine, as sharp and as clearly defined as though it had never left. "At least it's come back," Lam said. She sounded relieved. "But..."

Back. So there was a chance she would survive this. And if she didn't—then she'd be there, where it mattered. She'd have her answers—or would, once and for all, stop feeling the shadow of unsaid words hanging over her.

Diem Huong moved, as though through thick tar— the gestures she had been steeling herself to make since this morning.

"Lil'sis?" Lam asked, behind her. "You can't—"

Diem Huong knew what Lam would say: that they weren't sure. That the machine was half-built, barely tested, barely run through its paces. For all she knew, that door opened into a black hole; or in the right time, but into a vacuum where she couldn't breathe, or on the edge of a lava field so hot her lungs would burst into cinders. That they could find someone, or pay someone—or even use animals, though that would be as bad as humans, really, other living souls. "You know how it is," Diem Huong said. The door before her shimmered blue; and there was a wind on her face, a touch of cold like the bristles of a brush made of ice.

Answers. An end to her nightmares and the fears of

her confused dreams.

"I've known, yes," Lam said, slowly. Her hands moved; her arms encircled Diem Huong's chest. "But that's no reason. Come back, lil'sis. We'll make sure it's safe, before you go haring off into Heaven knows what."

There was still a chance. Diem Huong could still turn back—if she did turn back, she would see Lam's eyes, brimming with tears—would read the folly of what she was about to do.

"I know it's not safe," Diem Huong said; and, gently disengaging herself from Lam's arms, stepped forward—into a cold deeper than the void of space.

The Empress

Mi Hiep had been up since the Bi-Hour of the Ox—as old age settled into her bones, she found that she needed less and less sleep.

In these days of strife in the Empire, sleep was a luxury she couldn't afford to have.

She would receive the envoys of the Nam Federation at the Bi-Hour of the Horse, which left her plenty of time to discuss the current situation with her advisors.

Lady Linh pulled a map of the nearby star system, and carefully highlighted a patch at the edge of Dai Viet space. "The Nam Federation is gathering fleets," she said.

"How long until they can reach us?" Mi Hiep asked.

Lady Linh shook her head. "I don't know. The Ministry of War wasn't able to ascertain the range of their engines."

Mi Hiep looked at the fleet. If they'd been normal outsider ships, it would have taken them months or years to make their way inwards—past the first defences and straight to the heart of the Empire. If they'd been normal outsider ships, she would have deployed a mindship in their midst, moving with the deadly grace of primed weapons; a single pinpoint strike that would have crippled any of them in a heartbeat. But those were new ships, with the La Hoa drive; and her spies' reports suggested they could equal or surpass any mindships she might field.

"What do you think?" Mi Hiep asked, to her ancestors.

Around her, holograms flickered to life: emperors and empresses in old-fashioned court dresses, from the five-panels after the Exodus to the more elaborate, baroque style of clothing made possible by the accuracy of bots.

The First Ancestor, the Righteously Martial Emperor —hoary, wizened without the benefit of rejuv treatments, was the one who spoke. "This much is clear, child: they're not here to be friends with you."

The Ninth Ancestor, the Friend of Reform Emperor— named after an Old Earth emperor who had died in exile—frowned as he studied the map. "Assuming they can move through deep spaces—" he frowned at the map—"I suspect their target is the Imperial Shipyards."

"It makes sense," Lady Linh said, slowly, carefully. She looked older than any of the Emperors around her—and the Twenty-Third Emperor, who stood by her side, had once imprisoned her for treason. Mi Hiep knew well that none of them made her comfortable. "It would enable them to capture mindships—"

"Who wouldn't serve them," Mi Hiep said, more sharply than she'd intended. "They would still remember their families."

"Yes," Lady Linh said, weighing every word. She looked

at Mi Hiep, a little uncertainly: an expression Mi Hiep recognised as reluctance. It had to be something serious, then; Lady Linh had never been shy about her opinions—indeed, a misplaced memorial had been the cause of her thirty-year imprisonment.

"Go on," Mi Hiep said, inclining her head. She braced herself for the worst.

Lady Linh reached out to the screen. There was a brief lag while her implants synchronised with it—a brief flowering of colour, the red seal of an agent of the Embroidered Guard clearly visible; and then something else appeared on the screen.

It was a mindship—looking almost ordinary, innocuous at first sight. There was an odd protuberance on the hull, near the head; and a few more scattered here and there, like pustules. Then the ship started moving, and it became clear something was very, very wrong with it. No deadly grace, no ageless elegance; but the zigzagging, tottering course of a drunkard, curves that turned into unexpectedly sharp lines, movements that started closing back on themselves.

What had they done? Oh Ancestors, what had they done?

"It's a hijack," Lady Linh said, curtly. "Plug in a few modules at key points, and you can influence what the ship sees and thinks. Then it's just a matter of... fine manipulation."

There was silence, for a while. Then a snort from the First Emperor—who had taken the reign name

Righteously Martial after ascending to the throne over the ruins of his rivals. "That doesn't look like fine movements to me. If that's all they have against us..."

"That," Lady Linh said, gently, almost apologetically, "is almost a full year old. We've had reports that the technology has evolved, but no pictures or vids. It has been harder and harder to get Embroidered Guard undercover. The Nam Federation are suspicious."

Suspicious. Mi Hiep massaged her forehead. Vast movements of troops. A technology to turn their own mindships against them. The Imperial shipyards. It didn't take a Master of Wind and Water to know which way things lay.

"I see," she said. The envoys of the Nam Federation were not due for another two hours, but she already knew what they would say. They would make pretty excuses, and tell her about military manoeuvres and the necessity to maintain the peace on their fractious borders. And she would smile and nod, and not believe a word of it.

The Ninth Emperor turned, a ghostly shape against the metal panelling. "Someone is coming," he said.

The Sixteenth Empress raised her head, like a hound sniffing the wind. "Suu Nuoc. The child is in a hurry. He is arguing with the guards at the entrance. You had left orders not to be disturbed?"

"Yes, " Mi Hiep said, disguising a sigh. None of the ancestors liked Suu Nuoc—it wasn't clear if they thought he had been an inappropriate lover for an empress, or if they resented his lower-class origins. Mi Hiep was no fool: she had not promoted her former lover to the Board of Military Affairs. She had promoted a smart, resourceful man with utter loyalty to her, and that was what mattered. The ancestors could talk and talk and disapprove, but she was since long inured to being shamed by a mere look or stern talking-to.

Sometimes, she wondered what it would be like, to be truly alone—not to be the last descendent of a line of twenty-four emperors and empresses, her ancestors embodied into simulations so detailed they needed an entire wing of the palace to run. Sacrilege, of course; and the ancestors were useful, but still...

Of course, in truth, she was lonely all the time.

"Let him in," she sent to her bodyguards.

Suu Nuoc came in, out of breath; followed by the small, fist-sized avatar of *The Turtle's Golden Claw*. He took one quick glance around the room; and slowly lowered himself to the floor, his head touching the slats of the parquet.

"Your Highnesses," he said. The Emperors and Empresses frowned, the temperature in the room lowered by their disapproval. "Empress."

"General." Mi Hiep gestured at him to rise, but he remained where he was, his gaze stubbornly fixed on the floor. "Something bad?" she asked. The disapproval of the ancestors turned to her—her choice of words too familiar for a relationship between Empress and general.

Lady Linh used the commotion caused by Suu Nuoc's arrival to slowly and discreetly slide out of the room—correctly judging Mi Hiep's desire to be alone; or as alone as one could be, with twenty-four ancestors in her thoughts.

Suu Nuoc was in the mindset she'd jokingly called "the arrow"—clear and focused, with little time for propriety or respect. "Grand Master Bach Cuc has disappeared," he said. "The ship here says she had found the trail of the Citadel."

Oh.

"Close the door," Mi Hiep said to the guards outside. She waited for them to comply, and then turned her vision back into the room. She, too, was deadly focused, instantly aware of every single implication of his words. "You mean she would have found my daughter." She didn't need to name Bright Princess Ngoc Minh; that much was obvious. "And her Citadel."

Suu Nuoc was still staring at the floor—all she could see of him was an impeccably manicured topknot, with not a grey hair in sight. How young he was; thirty-five full years younger than her at least—even younger than Ngoc Minh. A lover to remind her of life and youth, which she'd lost such a long time ago; a caprice, to sleep with someone who was not one of her concubins—one of the few impulses she could allow herself.

"Did she leave out of her own volition?" Mi Hiep asked.

Suu Nuoc said nothing for a while. "I—don't think so. The timing is convenient. Too convenient."

"Then you think someone abducted her. Who?" Mi Hiep asked.

"I don't know," Suu Nuoc said. "I judged it pertinent to inform you ahead of every other consideration." She probably didn't imagine the faint sarcasm in his voice—he had never been one for common courtesies. Without her support, he would not have risen far at court.

"I see." There were many reasons people disapproved of Grand Master Bach Cuc and *The Turtle's Golden Claw*—thinking it unnatural that Bach Cuc should create a mindship who was part of the Imperial Family; fearing the return of Bright Princess Ngoc Minh and what it would mean to court life; even disapproving of her policy of war against the Nam Federation. Some advocated passionately for peace as the only way to survival.

She didn't begrudge them their opinion; the court would think as it desired, in a multiplicity of cliques and alliances that kept the scholars busy at each other's throats. But acting against Grand Master Bach Cuc...

"You will find her," she said to Suu Nuoc. "Her, or her corpse. And punish whoever has done this."

Suu Nuoc bowed, and left the room. *The Turtle's Golden Claw* didn't; it hovered closer, and said, in a calm and dispassionate voice, "Grandmother."

Mi Hiep nodded, noting with a sharp pang of perverse pleasure the discomfort of the gathered Ancestors at this acknowledgement of their relationship. "You are sure of what you told the General Who Read the Book of Heaven?"

The ship bobbed from side to side, thoughtfully. "Bach Cuc sounded confident enough. And she usually—"

Never sounded confident until it actually would work. Grand Master Bach Cuc had been cautious, unlikely to give in to fancies or announce results ahead of time solely to please her or the Board of Military Affairs. Everything she valued in a research scientist. "I see," Mi Hiep said. And, more softly, "How are you?"

Bach Cuc had been her Grand Master of Design Harmony, after all, the other grandmother *The Turtle's Golden Claw* could count on—the only family that would accept her and trust her. Mi Hiep's other children had not been so welcoming; and even Thousand-Heart Princess Ngoc Ha, who had carried *The Turtle's Golden Claw* in her womb, was not affectionate.

"I will be fine," *The Turtle's Golden Claw* said, slowly, carefully. "She is alive, isn't she?"

Mi Hiep could have lied. She could have nodded with the same conviction she'd bring into her interview with the envoys of the Nam Federation; but it wouldn't have been fair, or kind, to her granddaughter. "I hope she is."

"I see," *The Turtle's Golden Claw* said, stiffly. "I will help Book of Heaven in his investigations, then."

"It will be fine," Mi Hiep said—she only had an avatar, nothing she could hold or kiss for reassurance. Mindships were machines and blood and flesh; and they felt things as keenly as humans. "We will find her."

"Thank you, Grandmother."

Mi Hiep watched the ship go—she moved as smoothly as ever, but of course with an avatar it was difficult to determine what she truly felt, wasn't it? How worried or hurt or screaming she could be, inside?

She thought again of the picture Lady Linh had

presented; the crippled ship tricked into believing lies: hijacked, Lady Linh had said. Blinded until their only purpose was to serve their new masters—and she felt a fresh stab of anger at this. This wasn't the way to treat anyone, whether human or mindship.

But, if she couldn't halt the progress of the Nam Federation, this would happen. They would take ships and twist them into emotionless tools with forced loyalties.

They needed weapons: not merely war mindships, but something more potent, more advanced; something to strike fear into their enemies' hearts and dissuade them from ever entering Dai Viet space.

They needed Ngoc Minh's weapons—and Grand Master Bach Cuc and *The Turtle's Golden Claw* had been meant to find them for her.

The Citadel of Weeping Pearls had gone down in history as a refuge of peace; as a place that taught its denizens the serenity that came from not fearing anything—not bandits, or corrupt officials, or apathetic scholars. But such things—the serenity, the lack of fear—did not happen unless one had powerful means of defences.

Mi Hiep remembered visiting Ngoc Minh in her room, once—not yet the Bright Princess, but merely a gangly girl on the cusp of adulthood, always in discussion with a group of hermits she'd found on Heaven knew what forsaken planet or station. Her daughter had looked up from her conversation, and smiled at her: a smile that she'd always wonder about later, about whether it was loving or forced, fearful or genuinely serene. "You haven't come to your lessons," Mi Hiep had said.

"No," Ngoc Minh had said. "I was learning things here."

Mi Hiep had turned a jaded eye on the horde of hermits—all of them lying prostrate in obedience. As if obedience could make them respectable—their dresses varied from torn robes to rags, and some of them were so withdrawn from public life they were all but invisible on the communal network, with no information beyond their planet of birth showing up on her implants. "You will be Empress of Dai Viet one day, daughter; not an itinerant monk. The Grand Secretary's lessons are on statecraft and the rituals that keep us all safe."

"We are safe, Mother. Look." Ngoc Minh took a vase from a lacquered table: a beautiful piece of celadon with a network of cracks like a fragile eggshell. She pressed something to it—a lump that was no bigger than a grain of rice—and gestured to one of the monks, who bowed and took it out into the adjoining courtyard.

What in Heaven?

"This is pointless," Mi Hiep said. "You will go to your lessons now, child." She used the sternest voice of authority she could think of, the one she'd reserved for her children as toddlers, and for sentencing prisoners to death.

Ngoc Minh's face was serene. "Look, Mother." She was looking at the vase, too, frowning; some Buddhist meditation exercise, focusing her will on it or something similar—not that Mi Hiep had anything against Buddhism, but its philosophy of peace and acceptance was not what an Emperor needed. The Empire needed to fight every day for its survival; and an Emperor needed to choose the hard answers, rather than the most serene ones.

"If you think I have time for your nonsense—"

And then the vase winked out of existence.

There was no other word for it. It seemed to fracture along the seams of the cracks first, even as a soft radiance flowed from within it, as if it had held the pure, bottled light of late afternoon—but then the pieces themselves fractured and fractured into ever-smaller pieces, until nothing but a faint, colourless dust filled the courtyard; a dust that a rising wind carried upwards, into the empty space between the pagoda spires.

That was... Mi Hiep looked again at the courtyard: still empty and desolate, with the dust still rising in a fine, almost invisible whirlwind. "That's impossible," she said, sharply.

Ngoc Minh smiled; serene and utterly frightening. "Everything is possible, if you listen to the right people."

Looking back, that was when she'd started to be scared of her daughter. Scared of what she might do; of what she was thinking, which was clearly so different of what moved Mi Hiep. When Ngoc Minh had married her commoner wife, they'd fallen out; but the root of this last, explosive quarrel lay much earlier, in that tranquil afternoon scene where her small, quiet world bounded by ritual and habit had been utterly shattered.

She'd been a scared fool. Ngoc Minh had been right: anything that could safeguard the Empire in its hour of need was a boon. What did it matter where it came from?

It was time for war—and, if anyone had dared to harm her Grand Master of Design Harmony, they would feel the full weight of her fury.

The Younger Sister

Thousand-Heart Princess Ngoc Ha found Suu Nuoc and her daughter *The Turtle's Golden Claw* in the laboratory, at the tail end of what looked to be a long and gruelling series of interviews with everyone who had worked with Grand Master Bach Cuc. By his look, the Supervisor of Military Research was not having a good day.

Suu Nuoc acknowledged her with a brief nod. He was in one of his moods where he would eschew ritual in favour of efficiency, a frequent source of complaints and memorials against him. Normally, Ngoc Ha would have forced him to provide proper respect: she knew the importance of appearances, and the need to remind people of her place, as an Imperial Princess who was not the heir and only had honorary positions. But today, she needed to see something else.

The laboratory had been cleanly swept. The only virtual notes attached to objects were the ones with the seal of the army, officially warning people of the penalty attached to tinkering with an ongoing investigation. The shielded chamber with its harmonisation arch was swarming with bots, supervised in a bored fashion by an old technician with a withered hand. Ngoc Ha walked closer to the arch, but saw nothing that spoke to her.

"Mother!"

Of course, it was inevitable that *The Turtle's Golden Claw* would see her; and churlish of her, really, to ignore the ship. "Hello, daughter."

She knew she was being irrational when she saw the ship and didn't feel an ounce of maternal love—merely a faint sense of repulsion, a memory of Mother overwhelming her objections to the implantation of the Mind in her; the scared, sick feeling she'd had during most of the pregnancy; and the sense of exhausted dread when she realised that having delivered the Mind merely meant she was now the mother, stuck in that role until the day she died.

And, if she was honest with herself, it wasn't the pregnancy, or motherhood; or even the Mind that was the issue—it was that, seeing *The Turtle's Golden Claw*, she remembered, once again, that everything in her life had been twisted out of shape for her elder sister's benefit. Thirty years since Ngoc Minh had disappeared; and still she haunted Ngoc Ha's life. Even the name bestowed on Ngoc Ha by the court—the Thousand-Heart—was not entirely hers: she was named that way because she'd been filial and dutiful, unlike Ngoc Minh; because she had set up proper spousal quarters and regularly slept with her concubines—even though none of them brought her much comfort; or alleviated the taste of ashes that had been in her mouth for thirty years.

"I'm sorry about Grand Master Bach Cuc," Ngoc Ha

said to *The Turtle's Golden Claw.* "I'm sure General Suu Nuoc will find her. He's good at what he does."

"I'm sure he is," the ship said. Her avatar turned, taking in the laboratory. "Mother..."

Ngoc Ha braced herself—surely that sick feeling of panic in her belly wasn't what one was meant to feel, when one's child came to them with problems? "Yes, child?"

"I'm scared." *The Turtle's Golden Claw's* voice was barely audible. "This is too large. How could she disappear like that—with no warning, in the heart of the Purple Forbidden City?"

Meaning inside influence. Meaning court intrigues; the same ones she'd stepped away from after Ngoc Minh's disappearance. "I don't know," Ngoc Ha said. "But not everyone wanted Ngoc Minh to come back." Including her. She was glad to be rid of her sister the Bright Princess; to never have to be compared to her again; to never look at her and realise they had so little in common—not even Mother's love. But she wasn't the only one. Lady Linh was loyal to Mother; but the rest of the scholars weren't, not so much. Huu Tam, Mother's choice of heir, was dutiful and wise: not wild, not incomprehensibly attractive like Bright Princess Ngoc Minh; but safe. "Not everyone likes their little worlds overturned."

"What about you?" the ship asked, with simple and devastating perspicacity.

"I don't know," Ngoc Ha lied. She didn't know what she'd do, if she saw Ngoc Minh again—embrace her, shout at her—show her how much her life had twisted and stretched in the wake of her elder sister's flight?

"Princess," Suu Nuoc said. He stood by her, at quiet ease. "My apologies. I was busy."

"I can imagine," Ngoc Ha said.

"I'm surprised to see you here," Suu Nuoc said, slowly. "I thought you had no interest in what Grand Master Bach Cuc was doing."

"*The Turtle's Golden Claw* is my daughter," Ngoc Ha said.

"Of course," Suu Nuoc said. He watched her, for a while, with that intent expression on his face that made her feel pierced by a spear. "But that's not why you're here, is it?"

Ngoc Ha said nothing for a while. She watched the harmonisation arch, the faint blue light playing on its edges. "I did follow what Bach Cuc was doing," she said, at last. It had taken an effort: Grand Master Bach Cuc was proud, and sometimes unpleasant. "Because it mattered. To me, to my place in court." It wasn't quite that, of course. She'd needed to know—whether Ngoc Minh would come back. Whether what it had been worth it, the agony of being pregnant with *The Turtle's Golden Claw*; of giving birth in blood and pain and loneliness, all because her mother the Empress had ordered it.

"How did you think things would change?"

"I don't know," Ngoc Ha said. He was assessing her, wondering what she was worth as a suspect. It would have been amusing, if she hadn't been so nervous already. "I wanted to know what you'd found, but I assume you won't share it while you're still working out if I harmed her."

"Indeed," Suu Nuoc said. He made a small, ironic smile, and turned to embrace the lab. "Or perhaps I simply have nothing to share."

Ngoc Ha steeled herself—better to tell him now than later, or else she'd become a suspect like everyone else. And she knew better than to expect Mother's influence to protect her.

After all, it hadn't worked for Ngoc Minh.

"I know who saw Grand Master Bach Cuc last," she said, slowly, carefully. "Or close to last."

There was silence, in the wake of her words.

"Who?" Suu Nuoc asked, at the same time as *The Turtle's Golden Claw* asked "Why?"

Ngoc Ha smiled, coldly; putting all the weight of the freezing disapproval she sometimes trained on courtiers. "As I said—I was interested. In whether Ngoc Minh would come back. Someone came to me with information on the Citadel of Weeping Pearls."

Suu Nuoc's face had frozen into a harsh cast, as unyielding as cut diamonds. "Go on."

"He was a man named Quoc Quang, part of a small merchant delegation that was doing a run between the Scattered Pearls belt and the First Planet." She'd had her agents check him out: a small, pathetic man addicted to alcohol and a few less savoury things: hardly a threat, and hardly worth bringing to her attention, as the chief of her escort had said. Except that he'd said something about

Grand Master Bach Cuc.

Ngoc Ha had her work administering the Twenty-Third Planet—trying to bring Lady Linh's home back to the glory it had had, before the war, building graceful pagodas and orbitals from a pile of ashes and dust. But it was mostly a sinecure to keep her busy; and so, curious, she had made time to see Quoc Quang.

"He said his daughter was doing something to find the Citadel of Weeping Pearls—her and a woman named Tran Thi Long Lam, a Distinguished Scholar of Mathematics who returned home to mind her sick father. Apparently they thought they could do better than Grand Master Bach Cuc. He said—" she closed her eyes—"he needed to speak to Bach Cuc, to warn her."

"Warn her of what?"

"He wouldn't tell me."

Suu Nuoc's impeccably trimmed eyebrows rose. Ngoc Ha went on as though she'd seen nothing—after all, it was only the truth, and demons take the man if he didn't believe it. "And you believed him?" Suu Nuoc asked.

If Ngoc Ha closed her eyes, she could see Quoc Quang; could still smell the raw despair from him; could still hear his voice. "My wife disappeared with the Citadel. We were away, thirty years ago, when it happened. I apologise for my presumption; but I share your pain." And she hadn't been quite sure what to answer him; had let the emotionless, hardened mask of the imperial princess stare at him and nod, in a way that conveyed acceptance, and a modicum of disapproval. But, in her mind, she'd heard the dark, twisted part of her whisper: *what pain? You were glad Ngoc Minh disappeared.*

"He was very convincing," she said.

"So you sent him to Grand Master Bach Cuc," *The Turtle's Golden Claw* said. "And then... Bach Cuc disappeared."

Ngoc Ha shook her head, irritated at the implications. "Credit me with a little thoughtfulness, General. I sent guards with him; and though he had his interview with Bach Cuc without me, they watched him all the while, and escorted him back to his quarters in the Fifth District. The interview ended at the Bi-Hour of the Dog; Grand Master Bach Cuc was still within the Forbidden City long after that."

"It was the Bi-Hour of the Tiger," *The Turtle's Golden Claw* said. "Eight hours after that, at least."

"Right," Suu Nuoc said, in a way that suggested he didn't believe any of her intentions, or her words—he could be so terribly, so inadequately blunt some times. "And where is this—Quoc Quang now?"

She had checked, before coming. "He left this morning, with his ship. The destination he announced was his home on the Scattered Pearls belt. I have no reason to disbelieve that."

"Except that he left in rather a hurry after Bach Cuc disappeared?"

Ngoc Ha did her best not to bristle; but it was hard. "I checked. There was no extra passenger on board. Apart from him, nothing was taken onboard; not even a live woman or a corpse. The spaceport bots would have seen it otherwise." She felt more than heard *The Turtle's Golden Claw* tense. "Sorry. I had to consider all eventualities."

"That's all right," *The Turtle's Golden Claw* said. "I'm sure she's alive. She's resourceful."

Suu Nuoc and Ngoc Ha exchanged a long, deep look; he was as sceptical as her, but he wouldn't say anything. *For her sake*, she mouthed, and Suu Nuoc nodded.

"Fine." Suu Nuoc was silent, for a while. He stared at the harmonisation door, his face hard again; his gaze distant, probably considering something on the network via his implants. He had no mem-implants from ancestors—but then, Ngoc Ha, the unfavoured daughter of the family, had none either. "I will check, and let you know. "

"I see," Ngoc Ha said. And, to the ship, "Will you come with me to my quarters? We can have tea together."

"Of course!" *The Turtle's Golden Claw* said—happy to spend an afternoon with her mother, a rare occurrence for her. Once again, Ngoc Ha fought a wave of shame. She should be more present in the ship's life; should see her through her tumultuous childhood into adulthood—surely, it wasn't easy for her either, to have been born only for the purpose of finding someone else.

"Thank you for your evidence. You will be apprised, one way or another."

And she wasn't sure, as she walked away with the ship in tow, if she ought to be relieved or scared, or both.

The Officer

Suu Nuoc found the entrance to his chamber crowded with officials; and his mailbox overflowing with a variety of memorials from the court—from those chastising him for his carefree behaviour; to short messages asking for the results of his investigation. They were all so fresh from the Grand Secretarial office that he could still see the marks of the rescripts—it was bad, then, if even he could see it: the court had to be in disarray; the Grand Secretariat overwhelmed.

"General, general." A chorus of voices; but the ones that stood out belonged to Vinh and Hanh, two of the heir Huu Tam's supporters. "What happened to Grand Master Bach Cuc?"

"Are we safe?"

"How soon will we know?"

He closed his eyes, and wished, again, for the serenity that had come over him on the edge of the battlefield. It wasn't his world. It would never be his world—except that being a general was sleepless, dirty nights in the field with ten thousand bots hacked into his feeds, sending him contradictory information and expecting a split-second decision—and a pay that came too slight and too late to make any difference to his family's life. Whereas, as a court official, he could shower his relatives with clothes and food, and jewellery so beautifully fragile it seemed a mere breath would cut it in half.

And he could see the Empress—and hide the twinge of regret that took him whenever he did so; that deep-seated knowledge that no lover he'd had since her had ever filled the void she'd left.

It wouldn't last, of course. It couldn't last. The Empress was old, and the heir Huu Tam had no liking for her discards. Suu Nuoc would go home in disgrace one day, if he was lucky; or rot away in a jail somewhere if he was not. He lived with that fear; as he'd lived with the fear of losing his battles when he'd been a general. Most days, it didn't affect him. Most days, he could sleep quietly in his bed and reflect on a duty carried to its end.

And sometimes, he would look at these—at the arrogant courtiers before him, and remember they would be among the ones baying for his head after the Empress died.

"You have no business infringing on an imperial investigation," Suu Nuoc said. "The Empress, may she reign ten thousand years, is the one who will decide who is told what, and when."

Winces, from the front of the mob—Courtier Hanh was clearly sniggering at this upstart who could not even speak proper Viet; and her companion Vinh was working himself up for a peremptory answer. Meanwhile, in the background of Suu Nuoc's own consciousness—in the space where he hung motionless, connected to a thousand bots crawling all over the palace, a churning of activities—a taking apart of messages and private notes, an analysis of witnesses' testimonies, and a forensic report on the state of the laboratory.

Later.

He watched the courtiers Vinh and Hanh; dared them to speak. As he had known, they did not have his patience; and it was the florid, middle-aged man who spoke first. "There are rumours that Grand Master Bach Cuc is dead; and Bright Princess Ngoc Minh forever lost."

"Perhaps," Suu Nuoc said, with a shrug; and watched the ripples of that through the crowd. Neither Vinh nor Hanh seemed much surprised; though they could not have sweated more if it had been monsoon season. "That is none of my business. I will find Grand Master Bach Cuc; and then all will be made clear."

Again, he watched them—there was no further reaction, but the air was charged, as if just before a storm. Ngoc Minh's return was not welcome, then. Not a surprise. "I suggest you disperse. As I said—you will be apprised, one way or another."

Quick, furtive glances at him; he remembered he'd said much the same thing to Ngoc Ha—had he meant it with her as well? She was an odd one, the younger princess—mousy and silent, by all accounts a dull reflection of her elder sister. They might not have liked each other; but then again, would Bright Princess Ngoc Minh's return change anything for the worse to her situation? Ngoc Ha was isolated and in disfavour; and her prospects were unlikely to improve.

"You have heard the general. I would highly suggest you do disperse." A sharp, aged voice: Lady Linh, with a red seal of office imprinted into her clothes that made it clear she spoke as the Empress's voice; and flanked by two ghost-emperors—the Twenty-Third and the Thirteenth, if Suu Nuoc remembered correctly. The bots scuttling around her held the folds of her robe in a perfect circle.

Lady Linh gestured for him to enter his own room. "We need to talk," she said, gracefully.

Inside, the two dead emperors prowled, staring at the rumpled bed and the half-closed chests of drawers as if they were some kind of personal insult. Suu Nuoc did his best to ignore them as he offered tea to Lady Linh; but from time to time one of them would make a sharp sound in his throat, like a mother disapproving of a child's antics, and he would freeze, his heart beating like the wings of a caged bird.

Not his world. Did they know about his relatives—his cousins and aunts and uncles, greedily asking for favours from the court and never understanding why he couldn't grant them? Did they know about Mother, the poor bots-handler who held her chopsticks close to the tip and slurped her soup like a labourer?

Of course they did. And of course they would never forgive him that.

"Tell me," Lady Linh said. She shook her clothes; in the

communal network, the seal unfolded, spreading until it covered the entire room—a red filigree peeking underneath the painted floor, its edges licking at the base of the walls like flames. Bao Hoa. Keeper of the Peace.

Not so different from the battlefield, after all. Suu Nuoc shut off the bots for a moment, and called to mind all that they'd poured into his brain on the way back from Grand Master Bach Cuc's laboratory.

"She removed the implants herself," he said, finally. "It might have been under duress, all the same—for someone who was skilled with bots, it's a shoddy job—bits of flesh still sticking to the connectors, and a few wires twisted. Nothing irreplaceable, of course. If I were to guess—"

"Yes?"

"I think she was about to do something that needed absolute focus, and that's why the implants were removed. No distractions." No ancestors whispering in her mind; no ghostly manifestations of the past—he could only imagine it, of course; but it would be a bit like removing all his network syncs before leaping into battle.

"Go on," Lady Linh said, sipping her tea.

"Her correspondence is also interesting. The mails taper off: I think she was so busy with her work, so close to a breakthrough, that she wasn't answering as quickly as usual. I asked, but nothing seemed to be going on in her personal life—she had a girlfriend and a baby, but the girlfriend didn't see anything wrong."

"The girlfriend?" Lady Linh asked.

Suu Nuoc knew what she meant. The partner was often

the first suspect. "I don't think so," he said. He'd interviewed her—Cam Tu, a technician in a city lab, working so far away from court intrigues she hadn't even had any idea of who he was or what he wanted. "She wasn't in that night, nor was she aware of any of the context behind Grand Master Bach Cuc's research." It was—sad, in a way, to see this hunched woman with the child at her breast, and realise that Bach Cuc had deliberately shut her out of her life. But then again, he barely talked about the court when he did go home, so who was he to criticise? "Whatever happened to her, it was linked to the court."

"You talked of a breakthrough. The trail of the Citadel?"

"I think so, yes," Suu Nuoc said, slowly. "But that's not all." Something felt off to him; and he couldn't pinpoint what. "I'm still analysing the communications." It was the one thing the bots couldn't do for him; and he wasn't too sure he would be able to do it by himself either—where were the mem-implant ancestors when one needed them? A lot of it was abstruse mathematics; communications with other scientists in faraway labs, discussing methods and best practises, and screen after screen of equations until it felt his brain would burst. He was a soldier; a general; a passable courtier, but certainly never a mathematician. "There is... something," he said. He hesitated—looking at the two emperors, who had stopped walking around the room, and come to stand, like two bodyguards, by Lady Linh's side. "I'm not sure—"

Lady Linh set her teacup down, and looked at him for

a while, her seamed face inexpressive. "I was forty years old when I wrote my memorial," she said, with a nod to the Twenty-Third Emperor. "The one that sent me to trial. I've never regretted speaking up, Suu Nuoc; and you don't strike me as the type that would regret it, either." Her voice had lost the courtly accent; taken on the earthy tones of the outlying planets—he couldn't quite place it, but of course there were dozens of numbered planets, each of them with a multitude of provinces and magistrate fiefs.

The Twenty-Third Emperor spoke—still in the body of an adolescent, his youthful face at odds with the measured voice, the reasonable tone. "Speaking up is sometimes unwise," he said, with a pointed look at Lady Linh. "But one should always tell the truth to Emperors or their representatives."

"Indeed," Lady Linh's face was, again, expressionless. A truth that had sent her to jail for years; but that wasn't what Suu Nuoc feared.

He looked again at her, at the two emperors. Someone at court might be responsible for Grand Master Bach Cuc's disappearance; and they wouldn't take too kindly to efforts to make her reappear. Who could he trust?

It was a sacrilegious thought, but he wasn't even sure he could trust the dead emperors. But, because he would not disobey a direct order, or the intimation of one: "A man came to see Grand Master Bach Cuc. A merchant from the Scattered Pearls belt named Quoc Quang, who said he needed to warn her."

"Warn her? Why should he need to warn her? A peasant from the outreaches of the empire, to see the best Grand Master of Design Harmony in the Empire?" The Twenty-Third Emperor asked.

"I don't know," Suu Nuoc said. "But he did see her; and she disappeared after that. And then he disappeared, too. With your permission, I would like to go to the Scattered Pearls belt and question him." He'd thought long and hard about this: the Belt was a few days' journey from the First Planet via mindship; and, should he leave now, he wouldn't be far behind Quoc Quang.

"You assume he will return home," Lady Linh said.

"I see no indication he won't," Suu Nuoc said. His intuition—and he'd had time to learn when to trust his intuition—was that Quoc Quang was a witness, not a killer. He'd left plenty of time before Grand Master Bach Cuc disappeared; and the analysis of Bach Cuc's mem-implants showed, beyond a shadow of a doubt, that she'd removed them hours after her meeting with him. But whatever he'd said to her—it had struck home, because he had a record of her pacing the laboratory for half an hour after Quoc Quang had left, the only video he could grab from the feeds. After that, Bach Cuc herself had turned everything off.

Absolute focus. What had she been doing—or been forced into doing?

"I see," Lady Linh said. "You could send the Embroidered Guard to arrest him."

"Yes," Suu Nuoc said. "I could. But I'm not sure he

would arrive here alive." Fast, and blunt, like a gut punch. He saw the other Emperor, the Thirteenth, wince, his boy's face twisted and rippling like a face underwater.

"Court intrigues?" Lady Linh said, with a slight smile—Heaven only knew how many intrigues she'd weathered. On whose side did she stand? Not the Emperors, that was for sure—she was loyal to the Empress, perhaps, seeking only the return of Bright Princess Ngoc Minh; and yet, if Ngoc Minh did come back, her small, comfortable world where she was once more esteemed and listened to might vanish...

Lady Linh's eyes unfocused, slightly; and the red seal on the floor blinked, slowly, like the eye of some monster. "The Empress is informed. She agrees with your assessment. You will take *The Turtle's Golden Claw* to the Scattered Pearls belt, and interrogate this... Quoc Quang." Lady Linh's tone was slightly acerbic, and slightly too resonant: clearly she was still in contact with the Empress. "You will also take Thousand-Heart Princess Ngoc Ha with you."

What? Suu Nuoc fought the first imprecation that came to his lips. He didn't need a courtier with him; no, worse than a courtier, a princess who might have direct interest in burying her sister for good. *You can't possibly*— He took a deep, shaking breath. "Respectfully—"

"You disagree." Lady Linh's face was the Empress's serene, otherworldly mask, the one she wore when passing judgment; the same one she'd probably worn when exiling Bright Princess Ngoc Minh—though he hadn't been there to see it, of course, and he wouldn't have dared to ask her about those events. He was—had been—the lover of an Empress—pleasant, good in bed—but in no way a close confidante or a friend. He'd smiled, and never admitted how much it hurt to do so. "That is not a possibility, I'm afraid, general."

The Thirteenth Emperor leant over the table, his hand going through the teapot. "You will need someone versed in court intrigues." He'd been eight when he'd died; a boy, crowned by the ruling officials because they needed someone malleable and innocent. But in the implants he sounded older and wiser than both of them.

"I don't know where Ngoc Ha stands," Suu Nuoc said, stiffly.

"The Thousand-Heart Princess stands exactly where I need her, as I need her," Lady Linh said, except it was neither her voice, nor her expression.

Suu Nuoc bowed to the face of his Empress. "Of course. As you desire."

The Engineer

When she'd stepped through the harmonisation arch, Diem Huong had expected to die. In spite of what Lam had said—that the door did indeed open into the past—it could have led to so many places, an inhabitable planet, the middle of the vacuum, the deadly-pressured heart of a star...

Instead, she'd found herself in a wide, open corridor, with the low, warm light typical of space habitats—and the same, sharp familiar tang of recycled air in her nostrils. She turned, and saw the outline of the arch in the wall behind her, half-hidden beneath the scrolling calligraphy of Old Earth characters, spelling out words and poems she could not read.

So there was a way back, at least. Or something that looked like one.

The corridor was deserted and silent; she reached out, cautiously, for the wall, and felt the surface slightly give way to her; the text flowing around her outstretched hand, and then back again once she withdrew her hand. She was here, then; for real. Wherever this was, or whenever—but she remembered the smell, that faint memory of sandalwood and incense that was always home to her; and that sense of something large and ponderous always hovering in the background, that feeling of calm before words of condemnation or praise were uttered.

The citadel.

At last.

Mother...

She was back; standing in what would become the memories of her childhood home, and she didn't know what to feel anymore—if she should weep or shout or leap for joy. She simply stood, breathing it all in; savouring that feeling—for a moment, she was a child again, running down the corridors with Thuy and Hanh, reprogramming the kitchen's bots to manufacture fireworks they could set off in the little park; secure in the knowledge that she'd find Mother in the kitchen, her hands smelling of garlic and lime and fish sauce, and there would be rice on the table and broth boiling away on the stove, clinging to her hands and clothes like perfumed smoke.

A moment only; but in so many ways, she was no longer a child. She had lived six years on the Citadel in blissful ignorance; but ignorance was no longer bliss.

She needed to find Mother.

In the alcove by her side was a little altar to gods, with fruit and sticks of burning incense; she reached out and touched it, feeling the stickiness on her hands; the smell clinging to her clothes—whispering a prayer to whoever might be listening. Her touch set the mangos slightly askew, and she did not dare touch them again: superstition, but who knew what might help her, in this strange place that was neither now nor then?

Lam had given her a speech, once, about going back in time; about paradoxes and the fact she wouldn't be able to affect anything; but Diem Huong hadn't been paying enough attention. She wished she had. She wished she knew what would happen, if she met herself; if she harmed Mother, one way or another.

There was a stack of eight incense sticks by the altar: on impulse, she lit one, and kept one with her, for good luck. As she did so the screen above the altar came alive, asking her what she wanted—as if it had seen her, recognised her as a citizen, even though she didn't have the implants that would have enabled such a thing. She felt a thrill run through her, even as she told the screen to go dark.

The Citadel.

She wanted to run, to leap or scream—to rush to where Mother would be, to talk to her before it all vanished, before whatever miracle had brought her here vanished, before Lam somehow found a way to bring her back, before she died. She forced herself to stop; to hold herself still, as if Mother were still standing with her, one hand steadying her shoulder, her body very still besides her, absorbing all her eagerness to move. She needed...

She needed to think.

As she walked out of the corridor and onto a large plaza, she saw people giving her odd looks—she wore the wrong clothes, or walked the wrong way. As long as she didn't stop for long, it wouldn't matter. But, eventually...

Diem Huong closed her eyes. Once, thirty years ago, Mother had had her memorise the address and network contact for the house, in case she got lost. She'd had so many addresses and contacts since then; but this was the first and most treasured one she'd learnt.

Compartment 206, Eastern Quadrant, The Jade Pool. And a string of numbers and symbols that, input into any comms system, would call home.

The network implants she'd had as a child had been removed, six months after the Citadel vanished, when Father finally decided there was no coming back—when he started the long slow slide into drinking himself to death. She'd been too young to be taught by the hermits, and couldn't teleport or weaponise her thoughts, the way the others did.

She would need to ask someone for help.

The thought was enough to turn her legs to jelly. She wanted to keep her head down—she didn't need to be noticed as a time traveller or a vagrant, or whatever they'd make of her.

To calm herself down, she walked further. The plaza was flanked by a training centre: citizens in black robes went through their exercises—the Eight Pieces of Brocade, the same ones she still did every morning—under the watchful eyes of a yellow-robed Order member. At the furthest end, an old woman was staring at sand;

eventually the sand would blow up, as if there had been a small explosion; and then she'd stare at some other patch.

Who to ask? Someone who would take her seriously, but who wouldn't report her. So not the order member, or the trainees. The noodle seller on the side, watching negligently as her bots spun dough into body-length noodles, and dropped them into soup bowls filled with greens and meat? The storyteller, who was using his swarm of bots to project the shadows of a dragon and a princess on the walls?

Something was wrong.

Diem Huong looked around her. Nothing seemed to have changed: the noodle seller was still churning out bowl after bowl; the same crowd of people with multiple body mods was walking by, idly staring at the trainees.

Something—

She opened her hand. The incense stick she'd taken was no longer in it—no, that wasn't quite accurate. It had left a faint trace: a ghost image of itself, that was vanishing even as she stared at it, until nothing was left—as if she'd never taken it from the altar at all.

That was impossible. She ran her fingers on her hand, over and over again. No stick. Not even the smell of it on her skin. And something else, too: her hands had been sticky from touching the ripe mangoes on the altar, but now that, too, was gone.

As if she'd never touched them at all.

No.

That wasn't possible.

She ran, then. Heedless of the disapproving stares that followed her, she pelted back to the deserted corridor she'd arrived in—back to that small altar where she'd lit an incense stick and disturbed the fruit.

All the while, she could hear Lam's lecture in her mind—spacetime projections, presence matrices, a jumble of words bleeding into each other until they were all but incomprehensible—it had been late, and Diem Huong had been on her fiftieth adjustment to a piece's circuits—waiting by the side of the oven for her pattern to set in, absent-mindedly nibbling on a rice cake as a substitute for dinner. She hadn't meant to shut Lam out, but she'd thought she could ask again—that there would be another opportunity to listen to that particular lecture.

The altar was there. But other things weren't: the incense stick she'd lit had disappeared, and the fruit were back to the configuration she'd originally found them in. Her heart madly beating against her chest, she turned to the stack of incense sticks. Eight. Not seven, or even six. Eight, exactly the number she had found.

Bots could have done it, she supposed—could have brought back the missing sticks and straightened out the altar, for some incomprehensible reason—but bots couldn't remove a stick from her hands, or wash the mangoes' sugar from her skin. No, that wasn't it.

Her heart in her throat, she turned towards the space in the wall, to see the imprint of the arch.

But that, too, was gone, vanished as though it had never been.

***

You won't affect anything. That's the beauty of it. No paradoxes. Don't worry about killing yourself or your mother. Can't be done.

Later, much later, after Diem Huong had walked the length and breadth of the ship she was on (*The Tiger in the Banyan's Hollow*, one of the smaller, peripheral ones that composed the citadel), she measured the full import of Lam's words.

She was there, but not there. The things she took went back to where she had taken them; the food she tasted remained in her stomach for a few moments before it, too, faded away. She wasn't starving, though; wasn't growing faint from hunger or thirst—it was as if nothing affected her. In her conversations with people, their eyes would start to glaze after anything more simple than a question—forgetting that she stood there at all, that she had ever been there. She could speak again, and receive only a puzzled look— and then only puzzled words as the conversation started over again, with no memory of what had been said before. If she made no effort to be noticed—if she did not run or scream or make herself stand out from the crowd in any way, people's gazes would pause on her for a split second, and then move on to something else.

You won't affect anything, Lam had said, but that wasn't true. She could affect things—she just couldn't make them stick. It was as if the universe was wound like some coiled spring, and no matter how hard she pulled, it would always return to its position of equilibrium. The bigger the change she made, the more slowly it would be erased—she broke a vase on one of the altars, and it took two hours for the shards to knit themselves together again—but erasure always happened.

She moved plates and vases; turned on screens and ambient moods; and saw everything moving back into place, everything turning itself off, and people dismissing it as nothing more than a glitch.

At length, she sat down on the steps before the training centre, and stared at nothing for a while. She was there, and not there—how long would she even be in the Citadel? How long before the universe righted itself, and she was pulled back—into Lam's laboratory, or into some other nothingness? She stared at her own hands, wondering if they were turning more ghostly; if her whole being was vanishing?

Focus. She needed to. Focus. She looked at the screens: time had passed from morning to later afternoon, and the light of the ship was already dimming to the golden glow before sunset. Ten days before the Citadel vanished—nine and a half, now. And if she was still onboard...

If it was all for nothing, she might as well try to get the answers she'd come here for.

She got up, and went to one of the monks in the training centre: she picked one that was not teaching any students, and simply seemed to be sitting in a bench in the centre of the gardens, though not meditating either: simply relaxing after a hard day's work. "Yes, daughter?" he asked, looking at her. His eyes narrowed; wondering what she was doing there—she stood out in so many painful ways.

She had perhaps a handful of moments before he started forgetting that she was there. "I was wondering if you could help me. I need to get to *The Jade Pool.*" *Compartment 206, Eastern Quadrant.*

"You need to get elsewhere. Like the militia's offices," the monk said. He was still watching her, eyes narrowed. "You're not a citizen. How did you steal onboard?"

"Please," she said.

His eyes moved away from her; focused again, with the same shocked suspicion of the first look. "How can I help you, daughter?"

"I need to get to *The Jade Pool,*" Diem Huong said. "Please. I'm lost."

"That's not a matter for me. I need to report this to the Embroidered Guard."

She felt a spike of fear; and then remembered that no one would remember the report minutes after he had made it. "You don't need to do this." But his eyes, again, had moved away. It was useless. "Thank you," she said.

She walked away from him, feeling his eyes on the back of her head; and then, as time passed, the gaze lessen in intensity; and he looked right past her, not remembering who she was or that he had talked to her.

A ghost. Worse than a ghost—a presence everyone

forgot as soon as she left their life. A stranger in her own childhood, fighting against the spring of the universe snapping back into place. How was she ever going to get to Mother?

Lam. Help me. But it was useless. Her friend couldn't hear her. No one could.

Unless—

She wasn't really here, was she? She walked and took things like anyone else; except nothing stuck. She didn't have the implants everyone had; the ones that enabled them to teleport from one end of the Citadel to another; but she didn't really have any presence here, and yet she could still move things for a while; could still make screens respond to her.

Mother had talked about teleportation; and so had Father, in his cups or on the long nights when he railed against the unfairness of the world. It had been a matter of state of mind, they'd both said—of being one with the mindships that composed the Citadel; to see the world in their terms until everything seemed to be connected; until the world itself was but a footstep away. And of implants; but perhaps it wasn't about implants after all. Perhaps the rules of the past were different from those of the present.

Compartment 206, Eastern Quadrant. The Jade Pool.

Diem Huong closed her eyes, and concentrated.

The Empress

Mi Hiep prepared for her audience with the envoys of the Nam Federation as if she were preparing for war. Her attendants gave her the dress habitually reserved for receiving foreign envoys: a yellow robe with five-clawed dragons wending their ways across her body; a headdress bedecked with jewels. For the occasion, she had the alchemists alter her body chemistry to grow the fingernails of her two smallest fingers on each hand to three times their usual size, encasing them into long, gold protectors that turned her fingers into claws.

Huu Tam, her heir, waited by her side, decked in the robe with the five-clawed dragons that denoted his position. He looked nervous—she'd had him leave his usual mob of supporters at the door, and she knew it would make him feel vulnerable, a small child scolded for wrongdoing. Good, because he needed vulnerability; needed to be off-balance and question himself, to negate his tendency to be so sure of himself he didn't stop to consider what was best for the Empire. "Mother," he said, slowly, as Mi Hiep dismissed the attendants. "I'm not sure—"

"We've been over this," Mi Hiep said. "Do you think peace is worth any sacrifice?"

"We can't fight a war," Huu Tam said. He grimaced, looking for a moment much older than he was.

"No," Mi Hiep said. "And I'll do my best to see we don't. But we might have to, nevertheless."

Huu Tam nodded, slowly. He didn't like war; an occupation unworthy of a scholar. But he'd never been faced with decisions like these—wasn't the one who'd looked into Ngoc Minh's face, and sent ships towards the Citadel of the Bright Princess with the order to raze it—wasn't the one who'd lain down on his bed afterwards, waiting for the sound of his heartbeat to become inaudible again, for the pain against her ribs to vanish into nothingness.

He was her heir. He had to learn; and better early on, while she was still flesh-and-blood and not some disembodied, loveless ancestor on the data banks.

Mi Hiep sat on her throne, and waited—muting the communal network, as it would be a distraction more than anything else. She didn't need to see the banners above her head to know her full name and titles; and neither did she need access to her implants to remember everything Lady Linh and her advisors had told her.

The envoys would deny everything; dance and smile and pretend nothing was wrong. She, in turn, would have to make it clear that she was ready for war; and hint that she was not without resources, in the hopes the Nam Federation would seek easier prey.

Huu Tam moved, to stand on her left; and she

summoned, with a gesture, all of her ancestors' simulations, from the First Emperor to her mother, the Twenty-Fourth Empress: her chain of uninterrupted wisdom, all the way since the beginning of the dynasty, her living link to the past. Her true ancestors might well be dead, spun by the Wheel of Rebirth into other lives, but their words and personalities lived on, preserved with the same care Old Earthers had preserved poems and books.

They stood, on either side of her, as the envoys approached.

It was a small delegation: a florid, rotund woman flanked by a pinch-faced man and another, more relaxed one who reminded Mi Hiep of the hermits that had once attended Bright Princess Ngoc Minh. They both knelt on the floor until Mi Hiep gave them permission to rise: they remained on their knees, facing her; though there was nothing servile or fearful in their attitude. They looked around the lacquered pillars of the hall, at the proverbs engraved on the floor; and the exquisite constructs of the communal network—and their eyes were those of tigers among the sheep.

The woman's name was Diem Vy; after the exchanges of pleasantries and of ritual gifts, she spoke without waiting for Mi Hiep to invite her to do so. "We are pleased that you have accepted to receive us, Empress. I understand that you have expressed some... concerns about our excrcises."

Interesting. Mi Hiep expected dancing around the evidence, but Vy clearly did not care for this. Two could play this game. "Indeed," Mi Hiep said, wryly. "Massive movements of ships entirely too close to my borders tend to have this effect."

Vy's face crinkled in a smile—a pleasant, joyful one. Mi Hiep didn't trust her one measure. "Military exercises happen at borders," she said. "Generally, doing them near the capital tends to make citizens nervous."

"Fair point," Mi Hiep said. "Then this is nothing more than the norm?"

Vy did not answer. It was the other envoy, the serene-faced hermit—a man named Thich An Son, who answered. "A federation such as ours must always be ready to defend itself, Empress; and our neighbours have had... troubling activities."

"Not us," Mi Hiep said. If they were determined to be this transparent, she would not obfuscate. "We have no interest, at this time, in cryptic military games." Let them make of that what they willed.

Thich An Son smiled. "Of course not, Empress. We know we can trust you."

As if anyone here believed that, or the reverse. Mi Hiep returned the smile. "Of course. We will honour the treaties. We trust that you will do the same." And then, slowly, carefully, "I have heard... rumours, though."

Vy froze. "Rumours?"

Mi Hiep gestured to Lady Linh, who handed her a ghostly image of a folder stamped with the seal of the Embroidered Guard: a gesture merely for show, as she knew the contents of said folder by heart, and had no need to materialise it in the communal network. "Troubling things," she said, coldly, as if she already knew it all. "Ships that look like distorted versions of mindships."

"Copying designs is not a crime," Vy said, a touch more heatedly than the occasion warranted.

"Indeed, not," Mi Hiep said. "If that is all there is to it." She opened the folder in network space, making sure that it was as theatrical as possible—letting them see blurred images of ships and planets seen in every wavelength from radio to gamma rays.

"I assure you, Empress, you have no reason to be afraid," Vy said, sounding uncommonly nervous.

"Good," Mi Hiep said. "We are not, as you know, without resources. Or without weapons. We have, indeed, made much progress on that front, recently."

"I see," the hermit delegate Thich An Son said, his serene face almost—but not quite—undisturbed. The interview had not gone quite as planned. Good. "If I may be so bold, Empress?"

"Go ahead," Mi Hiep said.

"On an unrelated matter... there are rumours that you might be..." He paused, seemingly to pick his words with care—but really more for show than for anything else. "... considering changes at court?"

Reconsidering your choice of heir. Locating Bright Princess Ngoc Minh and her errant weapons. Mi Hiep glanced at Huu Tam, knowing everyone would do the same. Her son still stood by her side; with no change in his expression. He believed his sister dead for many years, and the lack of a body, or the recent search, had not changed his mind. At least, Mi Hiep hoped it hadn't; hoped he wasn't the one responsible for Grand Master Bach Cuc's disappearance. Whatever happened, his position at court was secure; and he knew it.

But, nevertheless, she had to make her point. She'd known she might have to do this beforehand; and had prepared both herself and Huu Tam for this moment.

"I believe there will be changes at court," Mi Hiep said, coldly. "Though if you're referring to my choice of heir, I see no reason to alter it."

The envoys looked at each other. "I see," Thich An Son said. "Thank you for the audience, Empress. We will not trouble you any further."

After they had left, Lady Linh approached the throne, and bowed. "It's bad, isn't it?" she said, without preamble.

Mi Hiep did not have the heart to chide her for the breach of protocol, though she could see a few of the more hidebound Emperors frown and make a visible effort not to speak up to censure either her or Lady Linh. "You said you didn't know about how far their fleet was."

"Yes," Lady Linh said.

"It's close," Mi Hiep said, trying to loosen the fist of ice that seemed to have closed around her stomach. Close enough that they would send these envoys—not the ones that would lie and prevaricate better, not the ones that would buy time. The Nam Federation had seen no reason to do so; and that meant they expected to make an imminent attack.

"You gave them something to think about," the Twen-ty-Fourth Empress said. Every time she spoke up, Mi Hiep's heart broke a little—it was her mother as a younger woman, but the simulation had preserved none of what had made her alive—simply collated her advice and her drive to preserve the empire into a personality the alche-mists had thought would be useful—never thinking that the child would became empress would need love and affection and all the support that could not be boiled down to appropriate words. It was one thing to know this for the old ones, the ones she'd never known; but for her own mother.... "They think you have the Bright Princess's weapons, or something close."

"But we don't," Huu Tam said. "Her Citadel and weap-ons died with her."

Mi Hiep said nothing for a while. "Perhaps."

"Ngoc Minh has been dead thirty years, Mother," Huu Tam's voice was gentle but firm. "If she could, don't you think she would have sent you a message? Even when she was in rebellion against the throne she sent you communications."

She had; and in all of them she was bright and fever-ish; with that inner fire Mi Hiep so desperately wanted to harness for the Empire; and couldn't.

Ngoc Minh, the Bright Princess, who only had to stare at things to make them detonate—her little tricks with vases and sand had expanded to less savoury things; to people who moved through space as though it were water, who would implant trackers and bombs on ship hulls as easily as if they'd been bots; to substances that could eat at anything faster than the strongest acid; and to teleportation, the hallmark of the Citadel's inhabitants. It had given Mi Hiep cold sweats, thirty years ago—the thought of an assassin materialising in her bedchambers, walking through walls and bodyguards as though they'd never been here...

But now she desperately needed those weapons; or even a fraction of them. Now the Empire was at risk, and she couldn't afford to turn anything down, not even her errant daughter.

"Has there been any word from Suu Nuoc?" she asked.

Lady Linh shook her head. "Some of your supporters are getting quite vocal against him," she said to Huu Tam.

He looked affronted. "I'm not responsible for what they choose to say."

Lady Linh grimaced, but said nothing. Mi Hiep had no such compunction. "They follow your cues," she said to Huu Tam. And Huu Tam didn't like Suu Nuoc—he never had. She didn't know if it was because of Suu Nuoc's bluntness; or because he had once been her lover and thus close in a way Huu Tam himself never had been.

"No accusations yet," the First Emperor said. "But a couple strongly worded memorials making their way upwards to the Grand Secretariat." He looked at Huu Tam with a frown. "Your mother is right. It is your responsibility to inspire your followers by your behaviour—" it was said in a way that very clearly implied said behaviour had not been above reproach, and Huu Tam visibly bristled—"or, failing that, reining them in with your authority."

"Fine, fine," Huu Tam said, sullenly. "But it's all non-sense, and you know it, Mother. It's not delusions that will help us. We need to focus on what matters."

"Military research and intelligence?" Mi Hiep asked. "That is also happening, child. Don't underestimate me."

"Never," Huu Tam said; and she didn't like the look in his eyes. He was... fragile in a way that none of her other children were; desperate for approval and affection, even from his concubines. But, out of all of them, he was the only one who had the backbone to rule an empire span-ning dozens of numbered planets. *The best of a bad choice*, as Suu Nuoc would have said—trust the man to always find the most tactless answer to everything. No wonder Huu Tam didn't like him.

"We'll get through this," Mi Hiep said, with more confidence than she felt. "As you said, we are not without resources."

Huu Tam nodded, slowly and unconvincingly. "As you say, Mother. I will go talk to my supporters."

After he was gone, Lady Linh frowned. "I will ask the Embroidered Guard to keep an eye on him."

He's innocent, Mi Hiep wanted to say. A little weak, a little too easily flattered; but surely not even he would dare to go against her will?

But still... One never knew. She hadn't raised him that way; and even he was smart enough to know that being family would not protect him against her wrath. He had seen her send armies against Ngoc Minh, when the threat of the Citadel had loomed so large in her mind she'd known she had to do something, or remain paralysed in fear that Ngoc Minh herself would act. She would weep if she had to exile or execute him, but she would not flinch. The Empire could not afford weakness.

Mi Hiep erased the folder from the communal network, and tried to remember what the next audience was—something about water rights on the Third Planet, wasn't it? She had the file somewhere, with abundant notes on the decision she'd uphold—the district magistrate had been absolutely correct, and the appeal would be closed on those terms. But every time she paused, even for a minute, she would remember her daughter.

Ngoc Minh had said nothing, when Mi Hiep had exiled her. She'd merely bowed; but though she'd lowered her eyes, her gaze still burnt through Mi Hiep's soul like a lance of fire, as if she'd laid bare every one of Mi Hiep's fears and petty thoughts.

Officially, the Bright Princess had disobeyed court orders once too many; had refused to set aside her commoner wife as a concubine, and set up proper spouses' quarters. It was one thing to take lovers, but fidelity to one particular person was absurd: those days, it wasn't the risk of infertility—alchemists' implantations had all but removed it—but merely the fact that no one could be allowed to own too much of an Empress's heart and mind. Favourites were one thing; wives quite another.

Unofficially—Mi Hiep had seen the vase, over and

over; the monks teleporting from one end to another of the courtyards; and thought of what this would do, the day it was turned against her.

"I will obey," Ngoc Minh had said. Had she known? She must have; must have guessed. And still she had said nothing.

"You're thinking of Ngoc Minh," the Twenty-Fourth Empress said.

"Yes. How do you know?" She wasn't meant to be so perceptive.

"I'm your mother," the Twenty-Fourth Empress said, with the bare hint of a smile; a reminder of the person she had been, once, the parent Mi Hiep had loved.

But she was none of those things. An Empress stood alone, and yet not alone—with no compassion or affection; merely the rituals and rebukes handed on by the ghosts of the dead. "I guess so," Mi Hiep said. And then, because she was still seeing her daughter's gaze, "Was I unfair?"

"Never," the First Emperor said.

"You are the Empress," the Sixteenth Empress said.

"Your word is law," the Twenty-Third Emperor said, his adolescent's face creased in a frown. "The law is your word."

All true; and yet none of it a comfort.

Lady Linh said nothing. Of course she wouldn't. She had been imprisoned once already, she wasn't foolish enough to overstep her boundaries again. What Mi Hiep needed was one of her lovers or former lovers—Suu Nuoc or Ky Vo or Hong Quy—to whisper sweet nothings to her; to hold her and reassure her with words they didn't mean or couldn't understand the import of. But there was a time and place for this; and her audience room wasn't it.

But then, to her surprise, Lady Linh spoke up, "I don't know. You did the best you could, with what you had. An Empress should listen to the wisdom of her ancestors, her parents and her advisors—else how would the Empire stand fast? This isn't a tyranny or a dictatorship where one can rule as whim dictates. There are rules, and rituals, and emperors must abide by them. Else we will descend into chaos again, and brother will fight brother, daughter abandon mother and son defy father. You cannot do as you will. Ngoc Minh... didn't listen."

No. She never had.

But that wasn't the reason why Mi Hiep had exiled her; that wasn't the reason why, years later, Mi Hiep sent the army to destroy her and her Citadel.

Perhaps the rumours were right, after all; perhaps Mi Hiep was getting old, and counting the years until the King of Hell's demons came to take her; and wishing she could make amends for all that had happened.

As if amends would ever change anything.

The Younger Sister

Ngoc Ha had always felt ill at ease on *The Turtle's Golden Claw*. It was there that she'd given birth; panting and moaning like some animal, bottling in all the pain of contractions until a primal scream tore its way out of her like a spear point thrust through her lungs— and she'd lain, exhausted, amidst the smell of blood and machine-oil, while everyone else clustered around the Mind she'd borne—checking vitals and blood flow, and rushing her to the cradle in the heartroom.

Alone. On *The Turtle's Golden Claw*, Ngoc Ha would always be alone and vulnerable, abandoned by everyone else. It was a foolish, unsubstantiated fear; but she couldn't let go of it.

But Mother had ordered her to come, and of course her orders were law. Literally so, since she was the Empress. Ngoc Ha swallowed her fear until it was nothing more than a tiny, festering shard in her heart, and came onboard.

The Turtle's Golden Claw was pleased, of course— almost beyond words, her corridors lit with red, joyous light, the poems scrolling on the walls all about homecomings and the happiness of family reunions. She gave Ngoc Ha the best cabin, right next to the heart-room—grey walls with old-fashioned watercolours of starscapes. Clearly the ship been working on decorating it for a while; and Ngoc Ha felt, once more, obscurely guilty she couldn't give her daughter more than distant affection.

She had taken an escort with her; and her maid—she could have kept them with her; but they would have brought her no company—not onboard this ship. So she left them in a neighbouring room, and stared at the walls, trying to calm herself—as *The Turtle's Golden Claw* moved away from the First Planet; and plunged into deep spaces—the start of their week-long journey towards the Scattered Pearls belt.

An oily sheen spread over the watercolours and walls, and everything began throbbing on no rhythm Ngoc Ha could name.

She logged into the network, and spent the next day watching vids—operas and family sagas, and reality shows in which the contestants sang in five different harmonies, or designed increasingly bizarre rice and algae confections with the help of fine-tuned bots. That way, she didn't have to look at the walls; didn't have to see the shadowy shapes on them; to see them slowly turning—watching her, waiting...

"Mother?" A knock at the door, though the avatar could have dropped straight into her cabin. "May I come in?"

Ngoc Ha, too exhausted and drained to care, agreed.

The small avatar of *The Turtle's Golden Claw* materialised next to her, hovering over the bedside table. "Mother, you're not well."

Really. Ngoc Ha bit off the sarcastic reply, and said instead, "I don't like deep spaces." No one did. Unless they were Suu Nuoc, who seemed to have a stomach of iron to go with his blank face. And at least they were normal ones—not the other, higher-order ones the ship had accessed during her search for Ngoc Minh. "I need to stay busy."

"You do," a voice said, gravely. To her surprise, it was Suu Nuoc—who stood at the open door of her room with two Embroidered Guards by his side. His face was set in a faint frown, revealing nothing. Hard to believe Mother had seen enough in him to—but no, she wouldn't go there. It had no bearing on anything else.

"I have vids," Ngoc Ha said, shaking her head. "Or encirclement games, if you feel like you need an adversary." She hated encirclement games; but she needed a distraction—they'd forced her to cut the vids; to pay attention to what was going on in the cabin...

Suu Nuoc shrugged. "You knew Grand Master Bach Cuc."

"A little," Ngoc Ha said, warily.

"How were her relationships with the rest of the court?"

Mother had said something about court intrigues, which had made no sense to Ngoc Ha. Then again, she supposed it was a case of the one-eyed man in the land of the blind—Suu Nuoc was a disaster at anything involving subtlety. "She was like you." She hadn't meant to be so blunt, but the faint smell of ozone, the slight yield to the air, the twisting shapes on the walls—they were doing funny things to her. "Blunt and uninterested in anything that wasn't her mission." And proud, with utter belief in her own capacities as a scientist in a way that could be off-putting.

"I see." Suu Nuoc inclined his head. "But she must have had enemies."

"She was no one," Ngoc Ha said. Oily shadows trailed on the wall, unfolded hands like scissors, legs like knives. They were going to turn, to see her... "But her mission—that made her friends, and enemies."

"Huu Tam?"

"Maybe." She hadn't had a heart-to-heart talk with Huu Tam since he became the heir—ironic, in a way, but then she and her brother had never been very close.

Unlike her and Ngoc Minh—a memory of fingers, folding her hands around a baby chick; of laughter under a pine tree in a solitary courtyard—and she breathed in, and buried the treacherous thought before it could unmake her. She'd never grieved for Ngoc Minh. Why should she, when she'd always believed her sister to be alive?

But sometimes, the hollows left by absence were worse than those left by death.

Focus. The last thing she needed was for this to intrude on her interview with Suu Nuoc—who would see her hesitation and interpret it as guilt or as Heaven knew what else. "If Ngoc Minh had come back, things would have changed. But you know this already."

"Yes." Suu Nuoc's face was impassive. "What I want to know is how they would have changed for you."

"I don't know," Ngoc Ha said, and realised it was the truth. Why did Mother want Ngoc Minh back—for a change of heir, with the wolves and tigers at their doors; or simply because she was old, and wanted reconciliation with the Bright Princess, the only child she'd ever sent away? "Who knows what Mother thinks?"

"I did, once," Suu Nuoc said. It was a statement of fact, nothing more.

"Then guess."

"That would be beyond my present attributions."

"Of course," Ngoc Ha said. "Fine. You want to know what I think? I didn't much care, one way or another." Untrue—the thought of seeing Ngoc Minh again was a knot in her stomach that only tightened the more she pulled about it. "I wasn't going to rise higher. We all know it, don't we? I don't have the ruthlessness it takes to become Empress." Huu Tam was too amenable to flattery—and his brothers were too weak and too inclined to play favourites. Ngoc Minh... Ngoc Minh had been intensely focused, dedicated to what she felt was right. But what was right had not included Mother's Empire.

"You might still not be very happy to be relegated to the background, again. She was your mother's favourite, wasn't she?" Suu Nuoc's voice was quiet. The shadows on

79

the walls were stretching, turning—reaching for her...
"Would you have been happy to see her back in your life?"

It wasn't that. She remembered a night like any other, when she had been tearing her hair out over an essay assigned by the Grand Secretary—remembered Ngoc Minh coming to sit by her—the rustle of yellow silk, the smell of sandalwood. She'd been busy by then; establishing her court of hermits and monks and mendicants, fighting the first hints of Mother's disapproval. "You're too serious, lil' sis," Ngoc Minh had said. "This isn't what matters."

Ngoc Ha wished she'd been smart enough then, to ask the unspoken question; to ask her what truly mattered.

"Leave her alone," *The Turtle's Golden Claw* said: a growl like a tiger's, sending ripples into the patterns on the wall.

Suu Nuoc looked surprised; as if a pet bird had bitten him to the blood.

"You know my orders."

"Yes," *The Turtle's Golden Claw* said. "Go to the Scattered Pearls belt and find and arrest Quoc Quang. Nowhere in this do I see a justification for what you're doing now, Book of Heaven."

Suu Nuoc's eyes narrowed at the over-familiar choice of nickname. "I do what needs to be done."

The Turtle's Golden Claw did not answer, but the atmosphere in the room tightened like an executioner's garrotte. Ngoc Ha, drained, merely watched—were they going to have it out? Such a stupid, wasteful idea to argue with a mindship in deep spaces. `

At length, Suu Nuoc looked at Ngoc Ha. "I will leave you then, Your Highness." He bowed, and left the room; and the tension in the air vanished like a burst bubble—leaving only the oily sheen and faint background noise of deep spaces around them, a cangue she could not escape.

"Thank you," Ngoc Ha whispered.

"It's nothing, Mother." *The Turtle's Golden* Claw's avatar materialised in the centre of the room, spinning left and right. "Just filial duty."

And what about motherly ones? Ngoc Ha suppressed the thought before it could undo her. No point in rehashing old wounds. "You wanted to find Ngoc Minh," she said. "How—"

The ship spun like glass blown by a master, gaining substance with every spin. "Grand Master Bach Cuc thought that deep spaces could be used—to go further. That there was something—" she stopped, picked her words again, "some place that was as far beyond them as deep spaces are to normal space. Places where time ceased to have meaning, where thirty years ago was still as fresh as yesterday."

"That's—" Ngoc Ha tried to swallow the words before they burnt her throat, and failed. "Esoteric babble. Unproved nonsense. I'm sorry." Grand Master Bach Cuc sounded as though she'd taken lessons from Ngoc Minh—like the Bright Princess, listened to hermits in some remote caves for far too long.

"That's all right." *The Turtle's Golden Claw* sounded disturbingly serene—Ngoc Minh again, standing in the courtyard by her room, smiling as Ngoc Ha shouted at her to behave, to see the plots being spun around her, the growing disenchantment of officials for an heir who did not follow Master Kong's teachings. "I knew you'd say that. That's why I brought you this."

She wanted nothing of this—-nonsense—she recoiled, instinctively, before realising that *The Turtle's Golden Claw* had given her nothing tangible: just a link to a database that hovered in the air in front of her. It was labelled "Quoc Tuan's personal files": Suu Nuoc's personal name, as grandiloquent as he had been obscure. "You can't."

"Of course I can." *The Turtle's Golden Claw* laughed, childish and almost carefree. "You forget—he stored everything in my databanks. I have the highest access credentials here."

Suu Nuoc would kill her—drag her so far down into the mud she'd never breathe again, with a few well-placed words in Mother's ears. "You can't do that," Ngoc Ha said, again. "I'm a suspect in that investigation."

"Are you?" The avatar of her daughter shifted; for a moment; became the head of a woman who took her breath away—a heartbreakingly familiar face with Mother's thin eyebrows and Ngoc Minh's burning eyes—a gaze that pierced her like a lance of fire.

No, Ngoc Ha thought, no. She had wished many things; some of them unforgivable—but she had never acted against anyone, let alone Grand Master Bach Cuc.

"I will leave you," *The Turtle's Golden Claw* said; and out of courtesy, opened the door and crossed through it rather than gradually fading away. The link remained in Ngoc Ha's field of vision, shifting to a turtle's scale, then a polished disc of jade, and other things of value beyond measure. *The Turtle's Golden Claw* really had a peculiar sense of humour.

Ngoc Ha stared at it for a while, and thought of the last time she had seen her sister—a brief message on the night before the Citadel vanished, asking news from her and assuring her everything was well. She dragged it up from her personal space, where she'd sat on it all those years, and stared at it for a while. Nothing seemed to have changed about Ngoc Minh in the years she'd been away from the First Planet—the same burning intensity, the same eyes that seemed to have seen too much. She had to know about Mother's army on its way to her; had to know that her Citadel would soon be embroiled in a war with no winners; but nothing of that had shown on her face.

Ngoc Ha had not answered that message. She had gone back to bed, telling herself she would think of something; that she would find words that would make it all better, as Ngoc Minh had once done for her. By morning, the Citadel was gone; and Ngoc Minh forever beyond her reach.

Where was the Bright Princess now—hiding somewhere she wouldn't be perceived as a threat to Mother's authority? Dead all those years? No, that wasn't possible. Ngoc Ha would have known—surely there was something, some shared connection remaining between them that would have told her?

And then she looked again at that last communication,

and realised, with a wrench in her stomach like the shutting of doors, that Ngoc Minh's face had become that of a stranger.

***

In the end, as *The Turtle's Golden Claw* had known, Ngoc Ha couldn't help herself. She took the link, and everything that the ship had given her, and started reading through it.

The bulk of the early pieces was Grand Master Bach Cuc's correspondence: her directions and discussions with her team; her memorials to Suu Nuoc; her letters asking other scientists on other planets for advice—buried in there, too was an account of *The Turtle's Golden Claw's* conception, implantation and birth, which Ngoc Ha gave a wide berth to—no desire to see herself as a subject of Bach Cuc's scientific curiosity, dissected with the same precision she'd put into all her experimental reports.

What interested her were the last communications. The earlier reports had been verbose, obfuscating the lack of progress. Those were terse to the point of rudeness—but it wasn't rudeness that leapt off the page—just a slow rising excitement that things were moving, that Bach Cuc's search would succeed at last, that she would be honoured by her peers for her breakthrough, her discovery of spaces beyond deep spaces where time and individuality ceased to have meaning.

Esoteric nonsense, Ngoc Ha would have said—except

that Grand Master Bach Cuc was one of the most pragmatic people she had ever met. If she believed it...

She read the correspondence from end to end, carefully. She wasn't a scientist; but unlike Suu Nuoc her broad education had gone deep into mathematics and physics, and the understanding of the rituals that bound the world as surely as Master Kong's teachings bound people. She could—barely—understand what it had been about from skimming the reports, and from Bach Cuc had told her, before and after the procedure of carrying *The Turtle's Golden Claw*.

And Bach Cuc had written a few reports already. She'd found a trail from the samples *The Turtle's Golden Claw* had brought back: trace elements that could only come from the Citadel's defences; clouds of particles from the technology Ngoc Minh had used to blast vases to smithereens in the courtyard of the palace. Bach Cuc had started to draw a plan for following these to a source; hoping to reconstitute the path the Citadel had taken after it had vanished from the world.

Hoping to find Ngoc Minh.

And then something had happened. Was it Quoc Quang? Ngoc Ha remembered the man's despair, his quiet, strong need to convince her that he needed to see Grand Master Bach Cuc. It had been that—the entreaty with no expectations—that had convinced her, more than anything.

What had he said? That, in the Scattered Pearls belt his daughter and Tran Thi Long Lam were working on something to do with the Citadel? She hadn't recorded the conversation for future use; but she remembered the name.

Tran Thi Long Lam. She had the profile on her implants: a scholar from the College of Brushes, the kind of brilliant mind that would never work well within the strictures of the imperial civil service. It was, in many ways, a blessing for her that she'd left to take care of her sick parent. But....

Yes, there were several communications from a Tran Thi Long Lam—or, more accurately, from her literary name, The Solitary Wanderer. Addressed to Grand Master Bach Cuc, and never answered—opened and read with a glance, perhaps? They didn't come from a laboratory or a university; or anyone Bach Cuc would have recognised as a peer—she could be a snob when she wanted to, and Lam might be brilliant, but she was also young, without any reputation to her name beyond the abandonment of what Bach Cuc would perceive as her responsibilities to science.

Ngoc Ha gathered them all, and stared at them for a while. The first sentences of the first one was "I humbly apologise for disturbing you. A common colleague of ours, Moral Mentor Da Thi from the Laboratory of Applied Photonics, has forwarded me some of your published articles on your research..."

No, Grand Master Bach Cuc would not have read very far in this kind of inflammatory statement, which barely acknowledged her as a superior before going on to question her research—the things that were going to make her fame and wealth. But Ngoc Ha was not Bach Cuc.

When Ngoc Ha was done reading, she stared at the wall; barely seeing, for once, the twisting, oily shadows that moved like broken bodies in slow motion. Warn Grand Master Bach Cuc, Quoc Quang had said, and now she understood a little of what he had meant.

Lam had been interested in Bach Cuc's research—possibly because whatever she was doing on her isolated orbital intersected it. She'd read it, carefully, applying everything she knew or thought she knew; and thought it worth writing to Bach Cuc.

Your research is dangerous.

Not because it could be weaponised; not because it was things mankind wasn't meant to know or any arrant outsider nonsense. No, what Lam had meant was rather more primal: that Grand Master Bach Cuc was wrong, and that it would kill her. Something about stability—Ngoc Ha read the second to last letter again—the stability of the samples *The Turtle's Golden Claw* was bringing back to the laboratory. Because they came from spaces where time had different meanings, they would tend to want to go back to those spaces. Lam thought this might happen in a violent, exothermic reaction—that all the coiled energy from the samples would release in one fatal explosion.

No, not quite. That wasn't what she'd said.

"Things disturbed have a tendency to go back to their

equilibrium point. In this particular case, I have reasons to believe this would be in a single, massive event rather than multiple small ones. I hold the calculations of this at your disposal, but I enclose an outline of them to convince you..."

Things disturbed. She hadn't been saying "be careful, your samples might explode". She had been saying "be careful, do not experiment on your samples". She'd told Grand Master Bach Cuc that the manipulations she was doing in her shielded chamber could prove fatal.

That was the warning Quoc Quang had passed on to Bach Cuc, with enough desperation and enough personal touch to make her pay attention.

Except...

Except Grand Master Bach Cuc was proud, wasn't she? Unbearably so. She had listened, but she'd done the wrong thing. Ngoc Ha would have put the project on hold while she worked out the risks, but she wasn't the one whose reputation had been impugned by a uppity eighteen-year-old and her drunken failure of a father.

She knew exactly what Bach Cuc had done. She had shown Quoc Quang out with a smile and her thanks— hiding the furious turmoil that had to have seized her at receiving such a warning. She had sat for a while, thinking on things—staring at the wall, just as Ngoc Ha was doing, trying to collect her thoughts, to think on the proper course of action.

And then she'd gone into the shielded chamber. She'd taken off her mem-implants because she'd needed absolute focus on what she was going to do; because she'd believed there might be a danger, but not to the level Lam was describing. Because she'd wanted to show the little outworlder upstart that she was wrong.

And it had killed her.

She had to—no, she couldn't tell that to *The Turtle's Golden Claw*—couldn't distress the ship without any evidence.

But she had to tell Suu Nuoc.

The Officer

Suu Nuoc was surprised by the Scattered Pearls belt. He couldn't have put his finger on what he'd expected—something both larger and less pathetic, more in tune with his mental image of what the Citadel had been?

It wasn't grand, or modern: everything appeared to have been cobbled together from scraps of disused metal, the walls looking like a patchwork of engineering, the communal network so primitive it required hard-wiring implants to have access to it—Suu Nuoc had refused, because who knew what they'd put in, if he allowed them access?

Beside him, Ngoc Ha was silent, her escort trailing behind her with closed faces. She had walked up to him earlier, on the shuttle taking them from the mindship to the central orbital, and had asked to speak with him in private. What she had then said...

He wasn't sure what to think of it. It sounded like the weakest chain of evidence he'd ever seen—wrapped into a compelling story, to be sure, but anyone could spin words, and especially a princess educated by the best scholars of the Empire. He'd read the research, and Lam's emails to Grand Master Bach Cuc—and had noticed none of this. But he knew his weaknesses; and unlike scholars, he didn't have any mem-implants to compensate his lack of education.

He'd thanked Ngoc Ha, and told her he'd think on it. "Don't tell my daughter," she'd said. For some reason, this had shocked him into silence—only after she'd gone had he realised that it was one of the only times she'd referred to the ship in those affectionate tones.

According to Ngoc Ha, Grand Master Bach Cuc was dead; which he wouldn't admit. It would mean a setback on the search for Bright Princess Ngoc Minh; at a time when they could not afford setbacks. He needed to be sure, before he told anyone of this—Heaven, he wasn't even sure Ngoc Ha was entirely innocent in this. She'd hated her sister: that much was clear from her own words.

Focus. He needed to do his duty to the Empress and the Empire; and flights of fancy were unhelpful.

The Scattered Pearls belt was governed by a council of elders, and a local magistrate who, like many of the low-echelon officials, looked stressed and perpetually harried. Yes, he knew of Quoc Quang, had always known he would be in trouble one day—it was the drugs, and the drinks, he'd never been the same since his wife's disappearance. Yes, he'd come back recently from a voyage into the heart of the Empire, and of course he would be happy to help the honoured General Who Read the Book of Heaven in any way required.

His obsequiousness, and the lack of attempt to defend

Quoc Quang, made Suu Nuoc feel faintly ill; but he tried not to let it show on his face. "Bring him to us," he said, more brusquely than he'd meant to, and was perversely glad to see the man flinch.

He watched as the magistrate intercepted a pale-looking clerk; and mentally tallied the time it was going to find Quoc Quang with their overstretched resources. Too much. "On second thought, cancel that order. Take us to him. It will be faster."

"He has a daughter, hasn't he?" Ngoc Ha asked, as the magistrate's clerks escorted them to another shuttle.

"Diem Huong," the magistrate said—with a frown. Clearly, he was about to add the daughter's behaviour to a list of perceived sins against the Empire, too. Coward; and a malicious one at that.

Suu Nuoc wouldn't stand for that. "Are you going to tell us about the daughter's failures, too?" he asked, conversationally.

The magistrate blanched—and Ngoc Ha winced. "No, of course not," he said—Suu Nuoc heard him swallow, once, twice, as his face went the colour of ceruse. "It's just that... Diem Huong has always been odd."

"Odd?"

"Obsessed," one of the clerks said, a little more gently than the magistrate. "Her mother was on the Citadel. She vanished when Diem Huong was six, and Diem Huong never quite recovered from it." Her eyes were grave, thoughtful. "If I may—"

"Go on," Suu Nuoc said, though he wasn't fooled. The

delivery was gentler, and meant more kindly; but it was the same, nevertheless.

Heaven, how he missed the battlefield, sometimes. Soldiers and bots wouldn't prevaricate, and whatever backstabbing might occur was short and clean.

"People break, some times," the clerk said. "Diem Huong... does her job, correctly. Helps her orbital with the hydroponics system. No one's ever had a complaint against her. But it's an open secret she and Lam, and a couple other youngsters, were obsessed with the Citadel."

"Lam? Tran Thi Long Lam?" *The Turtle's Golden Claw* asked.

The clerk, startled, looked at the small avatar of the ship—hadn't even noticed it floating by her side. "Yes," she said. "A graduate of the College of Brushes—"

Suu Nuoc tuned her out as she started to list Lam's qualifications. The orbital was proud of Lam, as they hadn't been of either Quoc Quang or his daughter—because Lam was the local girl who had succeeded beyond everyone's wildest dream; granted, she'd had to return home, but everyone understood the necessity of caring for a sick father. Lam was cool-headed and competent; and probably managed an important segment of her orbital—a position beneath her, but which she'd taken on without complaining on returning home. He'd seen it a thousand times already, and it was of no interest.

What mattered was Grand Master Bach Cuc, and Bright Princess Ngoc Minh.

He let the clerk drone on as their shuttle moved from

the central orbital to the Silver Abalone orbital—focusing again on the messages Lam had sent Grand Master Bach Cuc. Warnings, using a language too obscure for him to make them out. Was Ngoc Ha right? He didn't know. He knew that she was right in her assessment of Bach Cuc: that the Grand Master was proud of her achievements, and hungry for recognition. A young person like Lam, daring to question her... No, she wouldn't have listened to her. It was a wonder she'd received Quoc Quang at all; but perhaps she had not dared to refuse someone introduced by Ngoc Ha herself.

It galled him to even entertain the thought; because one did not speak ill of the disappeared or the dead; but he had not cared much for Bac Cuch.

Quoc Quang's compartment turned out to be a small and cosy one—the kitchen showing traces of use so heavy the cleaning bots hadn't quite managed to make them disappear, and a faint smell of sesame oil and fish sauce clung to everything.

It also did not contain Quoc Quang, or his wayward daughter. The aged aunt who lived with them—quailing in the face of the Embroidered Guard—said he had gone out.

"Running away?" *The Turtle's Golden Claw* asked.

Suu Nuoc shook his head. Getting drunk, more likely. "Scour the teahouses," he said. "Can someone access the network?" Without it, everything seemed curiously bare—objects with no context or no feelings attached to them. He ran a finger on the wok on the hearth, half-expecting information to pop up in his field of vision—what brand it was, what had last been cooked in it. But there was nothing.

The clerk nodded.

"Anything interesting?"

Silence, for a while. "A message from his daughter," she said at last. "Diem Huong. She says she's gone to work with Lam, at the teahouse."

Diem Huong. Long Lam. Suu Nuoc didn't even pause to consider. "Where is the teahouse?"

"I don't know—" the clerk started, and then another of her colleagues cut her off. "It's the old teahouse," he said. "Where the youngsters hang out, right by the White Turtle Temple on the outer rings."

"Take us there," Suu Nuoc said. "And keep looking for Quoc Quang!"

It was all scattering out—that familiar feeling he had before entering battle, when all the bots he was linked to left in different directions, and the battlefield opened up like the petals of flowers—that instant, frozen in time, before everything became rage and chaos; when he still felt the illusion of control over everything.

But this wasn't battle. This didn't involve ships or soldiers; or at least, not more than one ship. He could handle this.

He just wished he could believe his own lies.

***

The White Turtle Temple was a surprise, albeit a provincial one: a fragile construction of rafters and glass that stretched all the way to a heightened ceiling, a luxury that seemed unwarranted on an orbital—though the glass was probably shatter-proof, or not even glass. It had a quaint kind of prettiness; and yet... and yet, in its simple, affectless setup, it felt more authentic and warm than the hundred more impressive pagodas on the First Planet. When all this was over, Suu Nuoc should come there; should sit, for a while, in front of the statues of Quan Vu and Quan Am; and meditate on the fragile value of life.

The building next to the temple, squat and rectangular, had indeed been a teahouse—some tables were still outside, and the counter was lying in two pieces in the corridor. But that wasn't what raised Suu Nuoc's hackles.

The building glowed.

There was no other word for it. It was a faint blue radiance that seemed to seep through everything, making metal and plastics as translucent as high-quality porcelain—light creeping through every crack, every line of the walls until it seemed to be the glue that held it together. And it was a light that thrummed and throbbed, like...

He had seen this somewhere before. He gestured to the Embroidered Guard, had them position themselves on either side of the entrance. It didn't look as though there was any danger they could tackle—"unnatural light" not exactly being in their prerogatives. He'd been too cautious: he should have asked at least one of them to plug into the communal network—they would be blind to local cues. It had been fine when they'd just been on a mission to pick up a witness, but now...

He looked again at the light, wishing he knew what it reminded him of. That annoying buzz, just on the edge of hearing—like a ship's engine? But no, that wasn't it. How long had it been spreading? "I want to know if the monks of the temple filed a report," he said.

The magistrate looked at one of his clerks, who shook her head. "Not in the system."

Not so long, then. Perhaps there was still time.

But time for what?

"I can go in," a voice said. "Have a look." *The Turtle's Golden Claw.*

"Out of the question." Ngoc Ha's voice was flat; almost unrecognisable from the small, courtly woman who seldom spoke her mind so bluntly. "You have no idea what's in here."

"I'm not here," *The Turtle's Golden Claw* said. "Not really. It's just a projection—"

"There's enough of you here," Ngoc Ha said. "Bits and pieces hooked into the communal network. That's how you work, isn't it? You can't process this fast, this quickly, if you're not here in some capacity."

"Mother—"

"Tell me you're not here," Ngoc Ha said, relentless. Her hair was shot through with blue highlights—lifted as though in an invisible wind; and her eyes—her eyes seemed to burn. Did everyone look like that? But no, the clerks didn't seem affected to that extent. "Tell me there's no part of you here at all, and then I'll let you go in."

"You can't force me!" *The Turtle's Golden Claw* said. "Grand Master Bach Cuc—"

Ngoc Ha opened her mouth; and Suu Nuoc knew, then, exactly what she was going to say. He found himself moving then—catching the heated words Ngoc Ha was about to fling into her daughter's face, and covering them with his own. "The Grand Master is probably dead, ship. And what killed her might be inside."

There was silence, then; and that same unnatural light. At length the ship said—bobbing up and down like a torn feather in a storm—"She can't be. She can't— Mother— Book of Heaven—"

"I'm sorry," Ngoc Ha said.

"We're not sure—" Suu Nuoc started.

"Then there's still a chance—"

"Don't you recognise what this is?" Ngoc Ha asked.

"I've seen it before—"

Her voice was harsh, unforgiving. "It's the light of a harmonisation arch, General."

She was right. Suu Nuoc suppressed a curse. Harmonisation arches were localised around their surrounding frames—the biggest one he'd seen had been twice the size of a man, and already buckling under the stress. They certainly never cast a light strong enough to illuminate an entire building. Whatever was going on inside, it was badly out of control.

"I need your help," he said, to *The Turtle's Golden Claw*.

"Yes?"

"Tell me if the illumination is stable."

The ship was silent for a while; but even before she

spoke up, Suu Nuoc knew the answer. "No. The intensity has been increasing. And..."

More bad news, Suu Nuoc could tell. Why couldn't he have some luck, for a change?

"I would need more observations to confirm, but at the rate this is going, it will have spread to the entire orbital in a few hours."

"Do you know what's inside?"

"Not with certainty, no. But I can hazard a guess. Some explosive reaction that should have required containment—except that it's breached it," *The Turtle's Golden Claw* said.

Which was emphatically not good for the orbital, whichever way you put it. Suu Nuoc's physics were basic, but even he could intuit that. He took in a deep, trembling breath. The battle joined, again; the familiar ache in his bones and in his mind, telling him it was time to enter the maelstrom where everything was clean-cut and elegantly simple—where he could once more feel the thrill of split-second decisions; of hanging on the sword's edge between life and death.

Except it wasn't a battle; it wasn't enemy soldiers out there—just deep spaces and whatever else Bach Cuc had been handling, all the cryptic reports he'd barely been able to follow. Could he handle this? He was badly out of his depth...

But it was for the Empress; and the good of the Empire; and there was no choice. There had never been any choice.

He gestured to the Embroidered Guard. "Set up a perimeter, but don't get too comfortable. We're going in."

The Engineer

The world around Diem Huong shifted and twisted; and vanished—and, for a moment, she hung in a vacuum as deep as the space between stars, small and alone and frightened, on the edge of extinction—and, for a moment, she felt the touch of a presence against her mind, something vast and numinous and terrible, like the wings of some huge bird of prey, wrapping themselves around her until she choked.

And then she came slamming back into her body, into a place she recognised.

Or almost did. It was—and was not—as she remembered: the door to Mother's compartment, a mere narrow arch in a recessed corridor, indistinguishable from the other doors. From within came the smell of garlic and fish sauce, strong enough to make her feel six years old again. And yet... and yet, it was smaller, and diminished from what she remembered; almost ordinary, yet loaded with memories that threatened to overwhelm her.

Slowly, gently—not certain it would still remain there, if she moved, if she breathed—she raised a hand, and knocked.

Nothing.

She exhaled. And knocked again—and saw the tip of her fingers slide, for a bare moment, through the metal. A bare moment only, and then it was as solid as before.

She was fading. Going back in time to Lam's lab? To the void and whatever waited for her there?

No use in thinking upon it. She couldn't let fear choke her until she died of it. She braced herself to knock again, when the door opened.

She knew Mother's face by heart; the one on the holos on the ancestral altar, young and unlined and forever frozen into her early forties: the wide eyes, the round cheeks, the skin darkened by sunlight and starlight. She'd forgotten how much of her would be familiar—the smell of sandalwood clinging to her; the graceful movements that unlocked something deep, deep within her—and she was six again and safe; before the betrayal that shattered her world; before the years of grief.

"Can I help you?" Mother asked. She sounded puzzled.

She had to say something, no matter how inane; had to prevent Mother's face from creasing in the same look of suspicion she'd seen in the monk's eyes. Had to. "I'm sorry, but I had to meet you. I'm your daughter."

"Diem Huong?" Mother's voice was puzzled. "What joke is this? Diem Huong is outside playing at a friend's house. She's six years old."

"I know," Diem Huong said. She hadn't meant to say that; but in the face of the woman before her, all that came out was the truth, no matter how inadequate. "I come from another time," she said. "Another place."

"From the future?" Mother's eyes narrowed. "You'd better come in."

Inside, she turned, looked at Diem Huong—every time this happened, Diem Huong would wait with baited breath, afraid that this was it, the moment when Mother would start forgetting her again. "There is a family resemblance," Mother said at last.

"I was born in the year of the Water Tiger, in the Hour of the Rat," Diem Huong said, slowly. "You wanted to name me Thien Bao; Father thought it an inappropriate name for a girl. Please, Mother. I don't have much time, and I'm running out of it."

"We all are," Mother said, soberly. She gestured towards the kitchen. "Have a tea."

"There is no time," Diem Huong said; and paused, scrabbling for words. "What do you mean, 'we're running out of time?'"

Mother did not answer. She turned back, at last; looked at Diem Huong. "Oh, I'm sorry, I hadn't seen you here. What can I do for you?"

"Mother—" the words were out of Diem Huong's mouth before she could think; but they were said so low Mother did not seem to hear them. "You have to tell me. Why are you running out of time?"

Mother shook her head. "Who told you that?"

"You did. A moment ago."

"I did not." Mother's voice was cold. "You imagine things. Why don't you come into the kitchen, and then we can talk." She looked, uncertainly, at the door. She wouldn't remember how Diem Huong had got in—she was wondering if she should call the militia, temporising because Diem Huong looked innocuous, and perhaps just familiar enough.

Don't you recognise me, Mother? Can't you tell? I'm your daughter, and I need to know.

The corridor they stood in was dark, lit only by the altar to Quan Am in the corner—the bodhisattva's face lifted in that familiar half-smile—how many times had she stared at it on her way in or out, until it became woven into her memories?

"Please tell me," Diem Huong said, slowly, softly. "You said the Citadel still stood. You said you didn't know for how long." She should have started over; should have made up some story about being a distant relative, to explain the family likeliness—or even better, something official-sounding, an investigation by a magistrate or something that would scare her enough not to think. But no, she couldn't scare Mother. Couldn't, wouldn't.

Mother's face did not move. Diem Huong could not read her. Was she calling the militia? "Come into the kitchen," she said, finally; and Diem Huong gave in.

She got another puzzled look as Mother busied herself around the small kitchen—withdrawing tea from a cupboard, sending the bots to put together dumplings and cakes that they dropped into boiling water. "I'm sorry," Mother said. "I keep forgetting you were coming today."

"It's nothing," Diem Huong said. The kitchen was almost unfamiliar—she remembered the underside of the table; the feet of chairs; but all of it from a lower vantage. Had she played there, once? But then she saw the small doll on the tiling; and knelt, tears brimming in her eyes. Em Be Be—Little Baby Sister. She remembered *that*; the feel of the plastic hands in hers; the faint sour, familiar smell from clothes that had been chewed on and hugged and dragged everywhere.

Em Be Be.

"Oh, I'm sorry," Mother said. "My daughter left this here, and I was too lazy to clean up."

"It's nothing," Diem Huong said, again. She rose, holding the doll like a fragile treasure; her heart twisting as though a fist of ice were closing around it. "Really." She wasn't going to break down and cry in the middle of the kitchen, she really wasn't. She was stronger than this. "Tell me about the Citadel."

Mother was having that frown again—she was in the middle of a conversation that kept slipping under her. It was only a matter of time until she called the militia— except that the militia wouldn't remember her call for more than a few moments—or asked Diem Huong to leave, outright—something else she wouldn't remember, if it did happen.

Diem Huong watched the doll in her hands, wondering how long she had before it vanished; how long before she, too, vanished. "Please, elder aunt." She used the endearment; the term for intimates rather than another, more distant one.

"It's going to fall, one way or another," Mother said,

slowly, carefully. "The Empress's armies are coming here, aren't they?" She put a plate full of dumplings before Diem Huong, and stared, for a while, at the doll. "I have to think of this. We're not defenceless—of course we're not. But the harm..." She shook her head. "You don't have children, do you?"

Diem Huong shook her head.

"Sometimes, all you have are bad choices," Mother said.

Diem Huong carefully set the doll aside, and reached for a dumpling—it'd vanish too, because Mother had only baked it for her. All traces of her presence would go away, at some point; all memories of her. "Bad choices," she said. "I understand, believe me." The dumpling smelled of dough and meat and herbs; and of that indefinable tang of childhood, that promise that all would be well in the end; that the compartment was and forever would be safe.

All dust, in the end; all doomed to vanish in the whirlwind.

"Do you?" Mother's voice was distant. Had she forgotten, again? But instead, she said, "One day, my daughter will grow up to be someone like you, younger aunt—a strong and beautiful adult. And it will be because I've done what I had to."

"I don't understand," Diem Huong said.

"You don't have to." There were—no.

Mother—

There were tears in Mother's eyes. "No one leaves. We stand, united. Always. For those of us who can."

Mother, no.

Mother smiled, again. "That's all right," she said. "I didn't feel you'd understand, younger aunt. You're too young to have children; or believe in the necessity of holding up the world." And then her gaze unfocused again; slid over Diem Huong again. "Can you remind me what I was saying? I seem to be having these frightful absences."

She was crying; young and vulnerable and so utterly unlike Mother. Diem Huong had wanted.. reassurances. Explanations. Embraces that would have made everything right with the world. Not—not this. Never this. "I'm sorry," she said, slowly backing away from the kitchen. "I'm really sorry. I didn't mean—"

It was only after she passed it that she realised her arm had gone through the door. She barely had enough time to be worried; because, by the time she reached the street, the Embroidered Guard was massed there, waiting for her with their weapons drawn.

The Empress

Mi Hiep sat in her chambers, thinking of Ngoc Minh; of weapons; and of lost opportunities.

Next to her, a handful of ancestors flickered into existence. They cast no shadow: below them, the ceramic tiles displayed the same slowly changing pattern of mist and pebbles—giving Mi Hiep the impression she stood in a mountain stream on some faraway planet. "There is news," the First Emperor said. "Their fleet has jumped."

The La Hoa drive. "How far?" Mi Hiep asked.

"Not far," the Ninth Emperor said, fingering his bearded chin. "A few light-days."

Not mindships, then.

"They're going to jump again," Mi Hiep said, flatly. It wasn't a question.

"Yes," the First Emperor said. "They're still outside the Empire; but they won't be for long."

"There have been no news from the Scattered Pearls belt," the Ninth Emperor said, with a disapproving frown. "You shouldn't have sent Suu Nuoc on his own."

Again, and again, the same arguments, repeated with the plodding patience of the dead. "I sent Ngoc Ha with him."

"Not enough," the First Emperor said.

The door to her chambers opened; let through Lady Linh and Van, the head of the Embroidered Guard; followed by Huu Tam, and two servants bringing tea and dumplings on a lacquered tray. "You wanted to see us," Lady Linh said. She carried the folder Mi Hiep had toyed with, which she laid on the table—in the communal network, it bulged with ghostly files. Linh wouldn't have put anything in it unless she had a good reason.

"You have something," Mi Hiep said, more sharply than she'd intended to.

Huu Tam bowed to her: he didn't look sullen, for once—and Mi Hiep realised the glint in his eyes was all too familiar.

Fear. The bone-deep, paralysing terror of those on the edge of the abyss.

"I have intelligence," Van said, briefly bowing to Mi Hiep. Van, the head of the Embroidered Guard, was middle-aged now, with a wife and two children; but as preternaturally sharp as she had been, twenty years ago, when a look from her had sent scholars scattering back to their offices.

"I told her about the fleet," the First Emperor said, with a nod to Van. The Emperors liked her—she was scary and utterly loyal; and with the kind of contained imagination that didn't challenge their worldviews.

Mi Hiep gestured: the pattern on the floor became a dark red—the colour of blood and New Year's lanterns; and the pebbles vanished, replaced by abstract models.

Van opened the folder; spread the first picture on the table before Mi Hiep, over the inlaid nacre dragon and phoenix circling the word "longevity". It was an infrared with several luminous stains; and even with the low definition it was easy to see that they didn't all have the same heat signature. "This is what we have on the fleet," she said.

"The different stains are different ships?" Mi Hiep asked. She bent closer, trying to keep her heartbeat at a normal rate. They'd leapt, but not far—they wouldn't be there for a while.

Van took out two other pictures—still infrared, but close-ups in a slightly different band. One was a ship Mi Hiep had already seen—the squat, utilitarian design of Nam engineers, with little heat signature that she could see, everything slightly blurred and unfocused as if she watched through a pane of thick glass. The second one... She'd seen the second one, too, before; or its likeliness: twisted and bent and out of shape, something that had once been elegant but was now deformed by the added, pustulous modules.

They take ships, Lady Linh had said. Influence what they see and think, with just a few modules. They took living, breathing beings; with a family; with love—and they turned them into unthinking weapons of war.

"Their ships, and their hijacked mindships." She was surprised at the calm in her voice. She couldn't afford to be angry, not now. Van had laid the last picture on top of the first one; but in the communal network it was easy enough to invert the transparency layers so that she was staring at the fleet again.

Three hijacked mindships, twenty Nam ships. "Do you know anything about the mindships?" Huu Tam asked.

Van shook her head. "We have asked the outlying planets for any reports on missing mindships. One of them fits the profile of *The Lonely Tiger*, a mindship that disappeared near the Twenty-Third planet. We haven't apprised the family yet because we're not sure."

Not sure. What would it do to them—what kind of destruction would it wreak among them? Mi Hiep thought of *The Turtle's Golden Claw*; but it was different. She'd ordered the ship made for a cause; and that cause outweighed everything else; even the love she might have been able to provide.

"I see." Mi Hiep took a deep breath.

"We need to evacuate," Huu Tam said.

Mi Hiep nodded. "Yes. That too. But first, I need you to capture one of these."

"The mindships?" Van grimaced. "That's possible, but we'll sustain heavy losses."

"Yes," Mi Hiep said. The time for cautiousness; for dancing with diplomats and subtle threats, had since long passed. "I know. But they found a way to turn those against us; and to make them follow the fleet. Did they leap at the same time as the others?"

"Insofar as we can tell, yes," Van said. "Not as far as the others—it was very clear they were waiting for them to play catch-up."

Which meant they weren't as efficient as they could be, yet—that they couldn't harness the full potential of a mindship; leaping any distance they wanted when they wanted. Which was good news, in a way. "They're not up to speed yet," Mi Hiep said. "Which means we can study their shunts, and find a way to break them."

Van looked dubious. "With respect—"

"I know," Mi Hiep said. It wasn't so much the research—Grand Master Bach Cuc hadn't been the only genius scientist she'd had available, and there were plenty of war laboratories knowledgeable in Nam technology. "We don't have much time."

"And we'll pay a horrendous price." Van grimaced. She knew all about the calculus of cruelty, the abacuses that counted losses and gains as distant beads, ones that could not cause grief or sorrow or pain. "I'll send the order. You do realise this is a declaration of war." Huu Tam looked sick; but he said nothing. She hadn't misjudged him: alone of her surviving children he had the backbone to realise what must be done, and to carry it through.

"Then war it is," Mi Hiep said. "Round up the Nam envoys, will you? And send them home." The Galactic outsiders considered them untouchable; but both the Nam and the Dai Viet took a different position: they were their master's voices, and as such, the letters they bore, the words they uttered, were sacred. Their persons were not. But in this case, executions would not achieve anything; and it wasn't as though they had seen much that they could take back to their masters.

Van shrugged. She was more bloodthirsty than Mi Hiep. "As you wish."

The Ninth Emperor fingered the image, frowning. "Are they headed for the Imperial shipyards?" he asked.

"Too early to tell with certainty," Lady Linh said. She gestured, and another image—of the ships' trajectories—was overlaid over the old one. "The trajectory is consistent, though."

Mi Hiep watched the red line, weaving its way through the outer reaches of the numbered planets. There was not; or had ever been, much choice. "There are ships at anchor, in the shipyards?"

"And Mind-bearers," the simulation of her mother said. "They're heavily pregnant: they won't be in a state to travel."

"They will have to," Huu Tam said. His face was harsh—good, he was learning. One did not become Emperor of the Dai Viet by being squeamish. "How many are there?"

"Six."

"They'll fit onboard one of the ships." She spared a thought for what they were about to do; a shred of pity: she'd been pregnant, though not with a ship-mind—and she remembered all too well what it had felt like—deprived of sleep, gravid and unable to move without being short of breath. "Have them evacuate the station. Don't let the ship into deep spaces."

Everything got weird in deep spaces—and something as fragile as a foetus or the seed that would become a ship-mind would probably not bear it. "Probably"—no one had run experiments, or at least no one had admitted to it, though the Sixteenth Empress—who'd had a fondness for questionable science ethics—had come dangerously close to it in Mi Hiep's hearing.

Lady Linh was looking at something on the network; a list of names. "There are four ships at anchor in the yards," she said. "*The Dragons in the Peach Gardens. The Blackbirds' Bridge. The Crystal Down Below. The Bird that Looked South.*" She moved text around; and remained for a while, absorbing information. "The first two were here for refits. The others are young."

Young and vulnerable; still being taught by their mothers—children, in truth. Children whom she would have to send to war. Unless— "What about the military mindships?"

Van grimaced. "They're here already—we sent them a while ago. I've deployed them as protection."

"Good," Mi Hiep said. "Have the women and their birth-masters board *The Dragons in the Peach Gardens.*" An experienced ship was what they needed; not a younger, more panicked one who would be more likely to make mistakes. "Keep the young ships at anchor until the military ships have arrived." They wanted ships; and the building facilities of the yard; she had to provide bait. Like Van, she had since long got used to making ruthless decisions in a heartbeat: two young ships against a chance to turn the tide—against the protection of dozens of others? It was an easy decision.

"Oh, and one more thing," Mi Hiep said. "The shells

for those ship-minds?" The beautiful, lovingly crafted bodies, the shells of ships into which the Minds would be inserted after birth—months and months of painstaking work by the alchemists and the Grand Masters of Design Harmonies, fine-tuning every turn of the corridors to ensure the flow of *khi* would welcome the Mind within its new carapace. "Destroy them."

"Your highness," Van said, shocked. That stopped her, for a moment: she hadn't thought it was possible to shock Van.

To her surprise, it was Huu Tam who spoke. "The Empress is right. They've come here for our technologies. Let us leave nothing for them to grasp."

Technologies. Mindships. Weapons. How she wished they had something better-everything she'd feared from Ngoc Minh. If only they had the Bright Princess on their side.

But they didn't; and there was no point in weeping for what was past, or hoping for miracles. Whatever Suu Nuoc found in the Scattered Pearls belt, it would be too late. War had come to her, as it had thirty years ago; and, as she had done in the past, she met it head-on rather than let it cow her into submission. She nodded to Huu Tam. "You understand."

Her son bit his lip, in an all too familiar fashion. "I don't approve," he said. "But I know what has to be done."

Good. If they didn't agree on most things, they could at least agree on this. "Send word to Suu Nuoc," Mi Hiep said, ignoring Huu Tam's grimace. "Tell him we're at war."

The Younger Sister

Suu Nuoc took the head of a detachment of three men and stepped forward, into the maelstrom of light. Ngoc Ha watched him from behind one of the overturned tables—something crackled and popped when he stepped inside, like burning flesh on a grill; but he didn't seem to notice it.

He said something; but the words came through garbled—he moved at odd angles, faster than the eye could see at moments, slow enough to seem frozen at others, every limb seemingly on a different rhythm, like those nightmarish collages Ngoc Ha had seen as a child, a narrow, lined eye of an old Dai Viet within the pale, sallow face of a horse; the muzzle of a tiger with the smiling lips and cheeks of a woman—the familiar boundaries shattered until nothing made sense. Children's fancies, they had been; but what she saw now dragged the unease back into daylight, making it blossom like a rotting flower. "Suu Nuoc? Can you hear me?"

The Turtle's Golden Claw was hovering near the boundary, bobbing like a craft in a storm. "There's a differential," she said. "Different timelines all dragged together. If you gave me time—"

"No," Ngoc Ha said. She didn't even have to think, it came welling out of her like blood out of a wound.

Silence. Then *The Turtle's Golden Claw* said, sullenly, "I'm not a child, you know. You can't protect me forever."

"I wasn't trying," Ngoc Ha said; and realised, with a horrible twist in her gut, that this was true. She hadn't abandoned the ship—had played with her, taught her what she knew, but it had always been with that same pent-up resentment, that same feeling that the choice to have this child had been forced upon her—that Ngoc Minh was reaching, from wherever she was, and deforming every aspect of Ngoc Ha's life again. Thirty years. The Bright Princess had been gone thirty years, and in that time she had tasted freedom.

And loss; but the word came in her thoughts so quickly she barely registered it.

The Turtle's Golden Claw, heedless of her hesitations, was already skirting the boundary, making a small noise like a child humming—except the words were in some strange language, mathematical formulas and folk songs mingled together. "A to the power of four, the fisherman's lament on the water—divide by three times C minus delta, provided delta is negative—the citadel was impregnable, the Golden Turtle Spirit said, for as long as his claw remained in the crossbow, and the crossbow remained in the citadel..."

But the Citadel had fallen; and her sister was forever silent. Except, perhaps, inside; where all the answers awaited.

Ngoc Ha was hardly aware of moving—hardly aware of her slow crawl towards the boundary, until she stood by the side of *The Turtle's Golden Claw*—her hand trailing on what should have been air—feeling the hairs on her skin rise as if in a strong electrical current.

"Deep spaces," *The Turtle's Golden Claw* said. Her voice came out weird; by turns tinny and booming, as if she couldn't quite make up her mind as to which distance she stood.

"Here? That's not possible—"

"Why not?" *The Turtle's Golden Claw* asked; and Ngoc Ha had no answer.

Ngoc Ha pushed; felt her hand go in as though through congealed rice porridge. Deep spaces. Shadows and nightmares; and that sick feeling in her belly; that fear that they would take her; swallow her whole and change her utterly.

And yet...

Yet, somewhere within, were people who might know where her sister was.

"Can we go in?" she asked; and felt more than saw the ship smile.

"Of course, Mother."

***

Inside, it was dark; and cool—everything limned with that curious light—everything at odd angles, the furniture showing part of asteroids and metal lodes, and the flames of workshops; and legs and blank polished surfaces; and fragments of flowers lacquered on hardwood at the same time—different times, different point of views merged together in a way that made Ngoc Ha's head ache.

She looked at *The Turtle's Golden Claw*; but the ship was unchanged; and her hands were the same, veined and pale. Perhaps whatever had a hold there didn't apply to them; but she felt, in the background, some great pressure; some great presence awakening to their presence—a muzzle raised, questing; eyes like two supernovae turned their way...

"Here," *The Turtle's Golden Claw* said; and waited, patiently, for her to follow. She heard muffled noises: Suu Nuoc's voice, coming from far away, saying words she couldn't make out; and noises of metal against metal—and the same persistent hum in the background; and the shadows on the walls, the same as on the ship, stretching and turning and changing into claws...

She took a deep, shaking breath. Why had she charged in?

As they went deeper in, the furniture straightened up; things became... almost normal, save that everything seemed still charged with that curious, pent up electricity. "Time differentials," *The Turtle's Golden Claw* said. "Like the eye of the storm." She whispered something; after a while Ngoc Ha realised it was the same singsong incantations she'd said outside: "Integrate the quotient over the gradient lines—the princess' blood became pearls at the bottom of the river, and her husband committed suicide at her grave—four times the potential energy at the point of stability, divided by N..."

There was a door, ahead, and the light was almost blinding. Little by little—though it felt she was making no progress—they walked towards it, even as *The Turtle's Golden Claw* wove her equations together; her curious singsong of old legends and mathematics.

The lab reminded her of Grand Master Bach Cuc's: every surface covered with objects and odd construct—pieces of electronics, half-baked, discarded ceramics; the light playing over all of them, limning them in blue. It was filled with Suu Nuoc's escort, the Embroidered Guards standing ill at ease, wedged against bits and pieces of machines.

Ahead, another door: a harmonisation arch, the source of all the light, and Suu Nuoc, kneeling by the side of a young, panicked woman who was putting two bits of cabling together. "It's overloading," she said.

"Turn it off," Suu Nuoc said. He glanced up, and nodded at Ngoc Ha as she knelt by his side.

The Turtle's Golden Claw was still humming—more warily, avoiding the edges of the harmonisation arch. "You set up an access to deep spaces *here*?"

"As I said—" the young woman—Lam—took a brief, angry look at the mindship—"I didn't expect this to work!"

"Turn it off," Suu Nuoc said.

"I can't," Lam's voice was hard. "I have someone still inside."

"Diem Huong?" Ngoc Ha asked, and knew she was right. There was something about the arch; about what lay beyond it—there was something in the lab with them, that same vast presence she'd felt earlier, slowly turning towards them. "It's spreading to the orbital."

"Yes," Lam said. "I know. But I'm still not leaving Diem Huong in it."

The Turtle's Golden Claw followed the boundary of the harmonisation arch; slowly tracing is contours, whispering words Ngoc Ha could barely hear. "It's not stabilised, that's the issue."

"You can talk," Ngoc Ha said, more sharply than she'd meant to. "Grand Master Bach Cuc didn't stabilise anything either, and it killed her."

"We will not talk of Bach Cuc here," *The Turtle's Golden Claw* snapped.

Lam looked vaguely curious; but, through what appeared to be a supreme effort of will, turned her attention back to the door. Through the light Ngoc Ha caught glimpses and pieces—a hand, an arm; a fragment of an altar with incense sticks protruding from it; the face of a yellow-robed monk. Another place; another time. "What was it supposed to be?"

Lam finished clinching together her two cables—with no perceptible difference. She looked up, her face gleaming with blue-tinged sweat. "The Citadel. Diem Huong's always wanted to go back." She snapped her fingers; bots rose up from the floor, though they were in bad shape, missing arms and with live wires trailing from them. "A time machine sounded like a good idea, at the time."

A time machine. Summoning deep spaces on an

orbital. "And you thought Grand Master Bach Cuc was imprudent?"

"At least I'm still here," Lam snapped. "Which isn't, I understand, what happened with the Grand Master."

"Please stop arguing about Bach Cuc," Suu Nuoc said, in a low but commanding voice. "And turn this thing off. I don't care about Diem Huong. This is going to destroy the orbital."

"I'm not doing anything until Diem Huong walks out that door," Lam said.

Ngoc Ha stood, watching the door. Watching the light; and the presence without; and her daughter, the mind-ship, prowling around the machine like a tiger. A time machine. A window on the Citadel. On Ngoc Minh and her people and the distant past—the past that had twisted her life into its present shape and continued to hang over her like the shadow of a sword.

She reached out before she could stop herself—heard, distantly, Suu Nuoc's scream; felt Lam's arm pulling at her—but it was too late, she was already touching the arch—she'd expected some irresistible force to drag her in, some irreversible current that would have taken her to Diem Huong and the Citadel, amidst all the hurt she'd been bottling up.

Instead, there was silence.

Calm spread from the machine, like oil thrown on waves; a deafening lack of noise that seemed to still every-thing and everyone in its wake. And, like a huge beast lumbering towards its den, the presence that had been dogging Ngoc Ha ever since she'd entered the deep spaces turned its eyes towards her, and saw.

I am here.

It was a voice like the fires of stars torn apart, like the thunder of ships' engines, like the call of a bell in a temple beyond time.

I am here.

And it was a voice Ngoc Ha had heard, and never forgotten, one that rose in the holes of her heart, each word a twisting hook that dragged raw, red memories from the depths of the past.

Ngoc Minh.

The Engineer

Diem Huong stood, paralysed. The Embroidered Guards were staring at her; the commander raising a gun towards her. "There's been a report of an intruder here, harassing Madam Quynh."

Reports whose memories wouldn't last more than a few moments; but sometimes, a few moments was all that it took for a message to travel along a chain of command—and, like everyone else, the Embroidered Guards could teleport from the palace to any place in a heartbeat.

Diem Huong could teleport, too; but she was frozen, trying not to stare at the muzzle of five weapons aimed at her. They would shoot; and it didn't take that long for energy arcs to find their mark.

"Look," she said, "I can explain—" If she had enough time, they would forget her; why she was here, why she mattered. If she had enough time.

They all had their weapons raised; trained on her; and the commander was frowning, trying to see what to make of her. He was going to fire. He was going to—

There was only one thing for it.

Run.

Before she could think, she'd started pelting away from them—back towards the compartment, back towards Mother, who wouldn't recognise or acknowledge her, or answer any of her questions.

"Stop—"

At any moment, she would feel it; the energy going through her, the spasms as it travelled through her body—would fall to the floor screaming and twitching like a puppet taken apart—but still, she ran, towards the illusory, unattainable safety of a home that had since long ceased to be hers...

Run.

There was a wave of stillness; passing over the faces of the soldiers, catching them mid-frown and freezing them in place—an invisible wind that blew through the station, laying icy fingers on her like a caress.

In front of her, the door opened; save that it was wreathed in blue light, like that of the harmonisation arch—the wind blew through it, carrying through the smell of fried garlic and fish sauce, and jasmine rice—so incongruously familiar Diem Huong stopped. Surely that wasn't possible...

The wind blew through the door, carrying tatters of light towards it—each gust adding depth and body to the light, until the vague outline of a figure became visible—line after line, a shape drawn by a master's paintbrush—the outline of a face surrounded by a mane of black hair; of silk clothes and jade bracelets as green as forest leaves.

Lam. Had to be. Lam had finally found a way to rescue her.

But it wasn't Lam. The clothes were yellow brocade—for a moment only, and then they became the saffron of monks' robes; the hair was longer than Lam's, the face older and more refined—and the eyes were two pits of unbearable compassion. "Child," the woman said. "Come."

"Who are you?" Diem Huong asked.

The woman laughed; a low, pleasant sound with no edge of threat to it. "I am Ngoc Minh. Come now, there isn't much time."

Ngoc Minh? The Bright Princess? "I don't understand—" Diem Huong said, but Ngoc Minh was extending a hand as translucent as porcelain; and, because nothing else made sense, Diem Huong took it.

For a moment—a dizzying, terrifying moment—she hung again in the blackness, in the void between the stars, brushed by a presence as terrible as a mindship in deep spaces, something that wrapped huge wings around her until she choked—and then it passed, and she realised the terrible presence was the Bright Princess herself; that the wings weren't choking her; but holding her as she flew.

"It's going to be fine," the Bright Princess whispered, in her mind.

"Mother—"

There were no words in the darkness, in the void; just the distant, dispassionate light of stars; and the sound of beings calling to each other like spaceships in the deep.

There were no words; and no illusions left. Only kindness; and the memory of tears glistening in Mother's eyes.

"Your mother loved you," the Bright Princess said.

It still stands. But for how long?

It's going to fall, one way or another.

Sometimes, all you have are bad choices.

Make a stand, or be conquered. Kill, or be killed. Submit, or have to subjugate others.

Mother had sent them away—packing her daughter and her husband, hiding what it had cost her. She had known. She had known the Citadel had no other choice but to vanish; that Ngoc Minh would never fight against her own people. That she would gather, instead, all her powers—all her monks and hermits and their students, for one purpose only: to disappear where no one would ever find them.

"You told her," Diem Huong said. "What was going to happen. What you were going to do."

"Of course," the Bright Princess said. "It's a Citadel, not a dictatorship; not an Imperial Court. My word is law; but I wouldn't have decided something like this without asking everyone to make a choice. The cost was too high."

Too high. Mother had made her bad choice; to have her family survive; to have her daughter grow into adulthood. "Where is she?"

"Nowhere. Everywhere," the Bright Princess whispered. "Beyond your reach, forever, child. She made her choice. Let her be."

I didn't feel you'd understand, younger aunt. You're too

young to have children; or believe in the necessity of hold-ing up the world.

"I do understand," Diem Huong said, to the darkness, but it was too late. It had always been thirty years too late, and Mother was gone, and would not come back no matter how hard she prayed or worked. "I do understand, Mother," she whispered; and she realised, with a shock, that she was crying.

The Empress

Mi Hiep summoned Huu Tam to her quarters; in the gardens outside her rooms, where bots were maintaining the grottos and waterfalls, the pavilions by the side of ponds covered with water lilies and lotuses; the arched bridges covered by willow branches, like a prelude to separation.

"Walk with me, will you?"

Huu Tam was silent; staring at the skies; at the ballet of shuttles in the skies. His attendants walked three steps behind them; affording them both the illusion of privacy.

"We are at war," Mi Hiep said. In the communal network, every place in the gardens was named; everything associated with an exquisite poem. It had been, she remembered, a competition to choose the poems. Ngoc Minh had won in several places; but Mi Hiep couldn't even remember where her daughter's poems would be. She could look it up, of course, but it wouldn't be the same. "You're going to have to take more responsibilities."

Huu Tam snorted. "I'm not a warrior."

Two ghost emperors flickered into life: the first, the Righteously Martial Emperor, who had founded the dynasty in floods of blood; and the Twenty-Third, the Great Virtue Emperor, who had hidden in his palace while civil war tore apart the Empire. "No one is," the Twenty-Third Emperor said.

"I know." Huu Tam's voice was curt.

"You will need Van," Mi Hiep said. Then, carefully, "And Suu Nuoc."

He sucked in a breath, and looked away. He wouldn't contradict her—what child gainsaid their parents?—but he didn't agree. "You don't like him. You don't have to." She raised a hand, to forestall any objections. How was she going to make him understand? She had tried, for decades; and perhaps failed. "You like flattery, child. Always have. It's more pleasant to hear pleasant things about yourself; more pleasant never to be challenged. And more pleasant to surround yourself with friends."

"Who wouldn't?" Huu Tam was defiant.

"A court is not a nest of sycophants," the First Emperor said, sternly.

"Flattery will destroy you," the Twenty-Third Emperor—sallow-faced and fearful—whispered. "Look at my life as an example."

Huu Tam said nothing for a while. He would obey her, she knew; he was too well-bred and too polite. He wasn't Ngoc Minh; who would have disagreed and stormed off. He would talk to Suu Nuoc, but he wouldn't trust him. She couldn't force him to.

There was a wind, in the gardens; a ripple on the surface of the pond, bending the lotus flowers, as if a giant

129

hand from the heavens had rifled through them, discarding stems and petals—and the world seemed to pause and hold its breath for a bare moment.

Mi Hiep turned; and saw her.

She stood in the octagonal pavilion in the middle of the pond—not so much coalescing into existence, but simply here one moment, as if the universe had reorganised itself to include her—almost too far away for her to make out the face, though she would have recognised her in a heartbeat—and then, as Mi Hiep held a deep, burning breath, she flickered out of existence, and reappeared, an arm's length away from Huu Tam and her.

Huu Tam's face was pale. "Elder sister," he whispered.

The Bright Princess hadn't changed—still the same face that Mi Hiep remembered; the full cheeks, the burning eyes looking straight at her, refusing to bend to the Empress her mother. Her hair was the same, too; not tied in a topknot, but loose, falling all the way to the ground until it seemed to root her to the ground.

"Child," she whispered. "Where are you?" She could see the pavilion through Ngoc Minh's body; and the pink lotus flowers; and the darkening heavens over their heads.

Nowhere, whispered the wind. *Everywhere*.

"There are no miracles," Huu Tam whispered.

Yes. No. Perhaps, said the wind. *It doesn't matter.*

Mi Hiep reached out; and so did Ngoc Minh—one ghostly hand reaching for a wrinkled one—her touch was the cold between stars, a slight pressure that didn't feel quite real—like the memory of a dream on waking up.

Ngoc Minh smiled; and it seemed to fill up the entire world—and suddenly Mi Hiep was young again, watching an infant play in the courtyard, lining up pebbles and fragments of broken vases; and the infant looked up and saw her, and smiled, and the entire universe seemed to shift and twist and hurt like salted knives in wounds—and then she was older, and the infant older too; and she tossed and turned in her bed, afraid for her life—and she woke up and asked the army to invade the Citadel...

"Child...." I'm sorry, she wanted to say. The emperors had been right—Huu Tam had been right: it had never been about weapons or war; or about technologies she could steal from the citadel. But simply about this—a mother and her daughter, and all the unsaid words, the unsaid fears—the unsolved quarrel that was all Mi Hiep's fault.

Ngoc Minh said nothing, and merely smiled back.

I forgive you, the wind whispered. *Please forgive me, Mother.*

"What for?"

Greed. Anger. Disobedience. Good-bye, Mother.

"Child..." Mi Hiep reached out again; but Ngoc Minh was gone; and only the memory of that smile remained—and then even that was gone, and Mi Hiep was alone again, gasping for breaths that burnt her lungs, as the universe became a blur around her.

Huu Tam looked at her, shaking. "Mother—-"

Mi Hiep shook her head. "Not now, please."

"Empress!" It was Lady Linh and Van, both looking

grim. Mi Hiep took a deep breath, waiting for things to right themselves again—mercifully, none of the ghost emperors had said any words. "What is it?" she asked.

Van made a gesture; and the air between them filled with the image of a ship—battered and pocked through like the surface of an airless moon, with warmth—oxygen?—pouring out of a hole in the hull.

One of the Nam mindships.

"We have one," Van said. "But the rest jumped. Given their previous pattern, they'll be at the Imperial shipyards in two days."

Huu Tam threw a concerned look at Mi Hiep—who didn't answer. She didn't feel anything she said would make sense, in the wake of Ngoc Minh's disappearance. "How soon can you work on the ship?"

"We're getting it towed to the nearest safe space," Lady Linh said. "And sending a team of scientists on board, to start work immediately. They'll find out how it was done."

Of course they would. "And the shipyards?" Mi Hiep asked, slowly, carefully—every word feeling as though it broke a moment of magical silence.

"Pulling away, as you ordered." Van gestured again; and pulled an image into the network. The yards, with the shells of mindships clustered among them; and bots pulling them apart in slow motion, dismantling them little by little. As Van gestured, they moved in accelerated time—and everything seemed to disintegrate into nothingness. Other, whole ships moved to take the place of those she'd ordered destroyed: warships, bristling with weapons; and civilian ships, looking small and pathetic next to them, a bulwark against the inevitable. "They've already evacuated the Mind-bearers. The other ships are waiting for them."

There would be a battle—many battles, to slow down the Nam fleet in any way they could—waiting until they could gather their defences; until they could study the hijacked ship and determine how it had been done, and how it could be reversed. And even if it couldn't.. they still had their own mindships; and the might of their army. "We'll be fine, Mother," Huu Tam, softly. "One doesn't need miracles to fight a war."

No. One needed miracles to avoid one. But Ngoc Minh was gone, her technologies and her Citadel with her; and all that remained of her was the memory of a hand in hers, like the caress of the wind.

Where are you?

Nowhere. Everywhere.

Mi Hiep stood, her face unmoving; and listened to her advisors, steeling herself for what lay ahead—a long slow slog of unending battles and feints, of retreats and invasions and pincer moves, and the calculus of deaths and acceptable losses. She rubbed her hand, slowly, carefully.

Forgive me, Mother. Good-bye.

Good-bye, child.

And on her hand, the touch of the wind faded away, until it was nothing more than a gentle balm on her heart; a memory to cling to in the days ahead—as they all made their way forward in the days of the war, in an age without miracles.

The Younger Sister

Ngoc Ha stood, caught in the light—her hand thrust through the door, becoming part of the whirlwind of images beyond. She didn't feel any different; more as if her hand had ceased to exist altogether—no sensation coming back from it, nothing.

And then she did feel something—faint at first, but growing stronger with every passing moment—until she recognised the touch of a hand on hers, fingers interlacing with her own.

I am here.

She didn't think; merely pulled; and her hand came back from beyond the harmonisation arch; and with it, another hand and an arm and a body.

Two figures coalesced from within the maelstrom. The first, bedraggled and mousy, her topknot askew, her face streaked with tears, could only be the missing engineer.

"Huong," Lam said, sharply; and dropped what she was holding, to run towards her. "You idiot." She was crying, too; and Diem Huong let her drag her away. "You freaking idiot."

But the other one... the one whose hand Ngoc Ha was still holding, even now...

She had changed, and not changed. She was all of Ngoc Ha's memories—the hands closing hers around the baby chick; the tall, comforting presence who had held her after too many nights frustrated over her dissertations; the sister who had stood on the view-screen with her last message, assuring her all was well—and yet she was more, too. Her head was well under the harmonisation arch, except that there was about her a presence, a sense of vastness that went well beyond her actual size. She was faintly translucent, and so were her clothes, shifting from one shape to the next, from yellow brocade to nuns' saffron; the jewellery on her hands and wrists flickering in and out of existence.

"Elder sister." Nothing but formality would come past her frozen lips.

"Lil' sis." Ngoc Minh smiled, and looked at her. "There isn't much time."

"I don't understand," Ngoc Ha said. "Why are you here?"

"Because you called," Ngoc Minh said. With her free hand, the Bright Princess gestured to *The Turtle's Golden Claw*: the ship had moved, to stand by her side; though she said nothing. "Because blood calls to blood, even in the depths of time. "

"I—-" Ngoc Ha took a deep, trembling breath. "I wanted to find you. Or not to. I wasn't sure."

Ngoc Minh laughed. "You were always so indecisive."

Her eyes—her eyes were twin stars, their radiance burning. "As I said—I am here."

"Here?" Ngoc Ha asked. "Where?" The light streamed around her, blurring everything—beyond the arch, the world was still shattered splinters, meaningless fragments.

The Turtle's Golden Claw said, slowly, softly. "This is nowhere, nowhen. Just a pocket of deep spaces. A piece of the past."

Of course. They weren't like Grand Master Bach Cuc, destroyed in the conflagration within her laboratory; but were they any better off?

"Nowhere," Ngoc Minh said, with a nod. She looked, for a moment, past Ngoc Ha; at the two engineers huddled together in a corner of the laboratory, holding hands like two long-lost friends. "That's where I am, lil' sis. Everywhere. Nowhere. Beyond time, beyond space."

No. "You're dead," Ngoc Ha said, sharply; and the words burnt her throat like tears.

"Perhaps," Ngoc Minh said. "I and the Citadel and the people aboard—" she closed her eyes; and for a moment, she wasn't huge, or beyond time; but merely young, and tired, and faced with choices that had destroyed her—"Mother's army and I could have fought each other, spilling blood for every measure of the Citadel. I couldn't do that. Brother shall not fight brother, son shall not slay father, daughter shall not abandon mother..." The familiar litany of righteousness taught by their tutors, in days long gone by. "There was a way out."

Death.

"Nowhere. Everywhere," Ngoc Minh said. "If you go far enough into deep spaces, time ceases to have meaning. That's where I took the Citadel."

Time ceases to have meaning. Humanity, too, ceased to have any meaning—Ngoc Ha had read Grand Master Bach Cuc's notes—she'd sent *The Turtle's Golden Claw* there on her own, because humans who went this far *dissolved*, turning into the dust of stars, the ashes of planets. "You're not human," Ngoc Ha said. Not anymore.

"I'm not human either," *The Turtle's Golden Claw* said, gently.

Ngoc Minh merely smiled. "You place too much value on that word."

Because you're my sister. Because—because she was tired, too, of dragging the past behind her; of thirty years of not knowing whether she should mourn or move on; of Mother not giving her any attention beyond her use in finding her sister. Because—

"Did you never think of us?" The words were torn out of Ngoc Ha's mouth before she could think. Did she never see the sleepless nights, the days where she'd carefully moulded her face and her thoughts to never see Ngoc Minh—the long years of shaping a life around the wound of her absence?

Ngoc Minh did not answer. Not human. Not anymore. A star storm, somewhere in the vastness of space. Storms did not think whether they harmed you, or cared whether you grieved.

There isn't much time, she'd said. Of course. Of course no one could live for long, in deep spaces.

"Goodbye, lil' sis. Be at peace." And the Bright Princess withdrew her hand from Ngoc Ha's; turning back towards the light of the harmonisation arch, going back to wherever she was, whatever she had turned into—the face she showed now, the one that didn't seem to have changed, was nothing more than a mask, a gift to Ngoc Ha to comfort her. The real Ngoc Minh—and everyone else in the Citadel—didn't wear faces or bodies anymore.

But still, she'd come; for one last glimpse, one last gift. A moment, frozen in time, before the machine was turned off, or killed them all.

Be at peace.

If such a thing could ever happen—if memories could be erased, wounds magically healed, lives righted back into the proper shape, without the shadow of jealousy and love and loss.

"Wait," Ngoc Ha said; and Bright Princess Ngoc Minh paused—and looked back at her, reaching out with a translucent hand; her eyes serene and distant, her smile the same enigmatic one as the bodhisattva statues in the temples.

The hand was wreathed in light; the blue nimbus of the harmonisation door; the shadow of deep spaces where she lived, where no one could survive.

Nowhere. Everywhere.

"Wait."

"Mother—" *The Turtle's Golden Claw* said. "You can't—"

Ngoc Ha smiled. "Of course I can," she said; and reached out, and clasped her sister's hand to hers.

The Officer

From where he stood rooted to the ground, Suu Nuoc saw it all happen, as if in some nightmare he couldn't wake up from: Ngoc Ha talking with the figure in the doorway; *The Turtle's Golden Claw* screaming; and Lam cursing, the bots surging from the floor at her command, making for the arch.

Too late.

Ngoc Ha reached out, and took the outstretched hand. Her topknot had come undone, and her hair was streaming in the wind from the door—for a moment they stood side by side, the two sisters, almost like mirror images of each other, as if they were the same person with two very different paths in life.

"Princess!" Suu Nuoc called—knowing, with a horrible twist in his belly, what was going to happen before it did.

Ngoc Ha turned to look at him, for a fraction of a second. She smiled; and her smile was cold, distant already—a moment only, and then she turned back to look at her sister the Bright Princess; and her other hand wrapped itself around her sister's other hand, locking them in an embrace that couldn't be broken.

And then they were gone, scattering into a thousand shards of light.

"No," *The Turtle's Golden Claw* said. "No. Mother..."

No panic. This was not the time for it. With an effort, Suu Nuoc wrenched his thoughts back from the brink of incoherence. Someone needed to be pragmatic about matters, and clearly neither of the two scientists, nor the mindship, was going to provide level-headedness.

"She's gone," he said to *The Turtle's Golden Claw*. "This isn't what we need to worry about. How do we shut off this machine before it kills us all?"

"She's my mother!" *The Turtle's Golden Claw* said.

"I know," Suu Nuoc said, curtly. Pragmatism, again. Someone needed to have it. "You can look for her later."

"There is no later!"

"There always is. Leave it, will you? We have more pressing problems."

"Yes, we do." Lam had come back; and with her was the engineer—Diem Huong, who still looked as though she'd been through eight levels of Hell and beyond, but whose face no longer had the shocked look of someone who had seen things she shouldn't. "You're right. We need to shut this thing down. Come on, Huong. Give me a hand." They crouched together by the machine, handing each other bits and pieces of ceramic and cabling. After a while, *The Turtle's Golden Claw* drifted, reluctantly, to join them, interjecting advice, while the bots moved slowly, drunkenly, piecing things back together as best as they could.

Suu Nuoc, whose talents most emphatically did not lie

in science or experimental time machines, drifted back to the harmonisation arch, watching the world beyond—the collage of pristine corridors and delicately painted temples; the fragments of citizens teleporting from one ship to the next.

The Citadel. What the Empress had desperately sought. What she'd thought she desperately needed—and Suu Nuoc had never argued with her, only taken her orders to heart and done his best to see them to fruition.

But now... Now he wasn't so sure, anymore, that they'd ever needed any of this.

"It's gone," Diem Huong said, gently. She was standing by her side, watching the door; her voice quiet, thoughtful; though he was not fooled at the strength of the emotions she was repressing. "The Bright Princess took it too far into deep spaces, and it vanished. That's what really happened to it. That's why Grand Master Bach Cuc would never have found it. It only exists in the past, now."

"I know," Suu Nuoc said. Perhaps, if another of the Empress's children was willing to touch the arch—but his gut told him it wouldn't work again. Ngoc Ha had been close to Bright Princess Ngoc Minh; too close, in fact—the seeds of her ultimate fate already sown long before they had come here, to the Scattered Pearls belt. There was no one else whose touch would call forth the Bright Princess again; even if the Empress was willing to sanction the building of a time machine again, after it had killed a Master of Grand Design Harmony and almost destroyed an orbital.

"There!" Lam said, triumphantly. She rose, holding two bits of cable; at the same time as *The Turtle's Golden Claw* reached for something on the edge of the harmonisation arch.

The light went out, as if she'd thrown a switch; when it came on again, the air had changed—no longer charged or lit with blue, it was simply the slightly stale, odourless one of any orbital. And the room, too, shrank back to normal, the furniture simply tables and chairs, and screens, rather than the collage monstrosities Suu Nuoc and his squad had seen on the way in.

Suu Nuoc took a deep, trembling breath, trying to convince himself it was over.

The Turtle's Golden Claw drifted back to the machine— now nothing more than a rectangle with a de-activated harmonisation arch, looking small and pathetic, and altogether too diminished to have caused so much trouble. "I'll find her," she said. "Somewhere in deep spaces..."

Suu Nuoc said nothing. He'd have to gather them all; to bring them back to the First Planet, so they could be debriefed—so he could explain to the Empress why she had lost a second daughter. And—if she still would have him, when it was all accounted for—he would have to help her fight a war.

But, for now, he watched the harmonisation arch; and remembered what he had seen through it. The past. The Citadel, like some fabled underground treasure. Ghostly apparitions, like myths and fairytales—nothing to build a life or a war strategy on.

The present was all that mattered. The past's grievous wounds had to close, or to be ignored; and the future's war and the baying of wolves could only be distant worries. He would stand where he had always stood; by his Empress's side, to guide the Empire forward for as long as she would have him.

The Citadel was gone, and so were its miracles—but wasn't it for the best, after all?

About the Author

Aliette de Bodard lives and works in Paris, where she has a day job as a System Engineer. She studied Computer Science and Applied Mathematics, but moonlights as a writer of speculative fiction. She is the author of the critically acclaimed *Obsidian and Blood* trilogy of Aztec noir fantasies, as well as numerous short stories, which garnered her two Nebula Awards, a Locus Award and a British Science Fiction Association Award.

Works include *The House of Shattered Wings* (2015 British Science Fiction Association Award), a novel set in a turn-of-the-century Paris devastated by a magical war, and its standalone sequel *The House of Binding Thorns*. She lives in Paris with her family, in a flat with more computers than warm bodies, and a set of Lovecraftian tentacled plants intent on taking over the place.

This novella is set in the same universe as her Vietnamese space opera *On a Red Station Drifting*.

Visit her website www.aliettedebodard.com for short fiction set in the same universe as this book, as well as Vietnamese and French recipes.

Read on for an excerpt of *On A Red Station, Drifting,* a short novel set in the same universe as this book and featuring a younger Lady Linh...

Linh arrived on Prosper Station blown by the winds of war, amidst a ship full of refugees who huddled together, speaking tearfully of the invading armies: the war between the rebel lords and the Empire had escalated, and their war-kites had laid waste to entire planets.

Linh kept her distance, not wanting to draw attention to herself on the way there; but, when they disembarked from the mindship and joined the immigration queue, she found herself behind an old woman in a shawl, who glanced fearfully around her, as if she expected soldiers to come out of the shadows at any moment. Bent and bowed, she looked so much like Linh's long-dead mother that Linh found herself instinctively reaching out.

"It's going to be all right, Madam," she said.

The woman looked at her: past her, in that particular way of old people whose mind wasn't steady anymore. "They'll come here," she whispered, her eyes boring into Linh's, uncomfortably bright and feverish. "There is no escape."

"We're safe," Linh said.

The woman looked sceptical. Linh drew herself to her full height, calling on a hint of the dignity and poise she'd taken when heading her tribunal sessions. "We are the children of the Emperor, and he will protect us."

The old woman looked at her for a while, as if seeing her for the first time. "If you say so, child."

"I know it to be true," Linh said. She mouthed the words, the platitudes, effortlessly, as though she believed them: a good scholar, a good magistrate, able to engage in any argument, no matter how trivial or nonsensical. Of course she knew the Emperor had no desire to engage the rebel lords; that he was young, and badly advised, and would prefer to retreat. She knew all the words. After all, her denunciation of that policy was what had tarred her with the red ink of criminals; sent her on the run to this spirits-forsaken place with nothing but her wits to rely on.

The old woman had turned away. They were almost at the beginning of the queue now, and Linh could see three men in livery, checking papers and directing refugees into the station itself. Linh took a deep breath, bracing herself. Every instinct she had called for her to slip through like the other refugees.

Every instinct but one, and she could feel, through the mem-implants, her First Ancestor Thanh Thuy's presence, the old woman as strong and querulous as ever, reminding her that ties of blood held up Heaven and Earth; that even though Linh didn't know Prosper Station and had never met the family, they were still relatives, and entitled to far more than minimal courtesies.

And, of course, as usual, First Ancestor was right.

Linh shook her head, shaking off the slight dissociation that always came with mem-implants. It was becoming harder and harder to tell implants from her own mind, a side-effect of being so good with them.

She waited until they'd checked papers, and given her the permissions that would allow her to access the trance, Prosper's internal network. Then, when the queue of refugees had wandered away in search of their fortune, she sought someone in charge, who turned out to be a young man with a quivering voice, barely old enough to have passed his exams.

"I am Lê Thi Linh," she said. Lê, like all Dai Viet names, was common. But the way she held herself, and her utter certainty, was enough to shake him.

She stood silent and unmoving as he dragged her into the trance: she got a brief flash of his credentials as Keeper of the Outer Gates for Prosper Station, and an even briefer flash of his family tree, the line of his greater ancestors lighting up in red, warm tones, all the way up until it intersected her own lineage. A cousin, somewhat removed. Hardly surprising, as most of Prosper Station came, ultimately, from the same stock that had bred her: Lê Thi Phuoc, who had borne in her womb the Honoured Ancestress and Her four human siblings.

"I see." She could see him swallow, convulsively, could track the beads of sweat on his pale skin: everything thrown into merciless clarity, as if he were a witness before her tribunal. "Welcome, Aunt Linh. I'll take you to the Inner Quarters."

She followed him, not into the refugee hall, but into another, smaller corridor and then another, until they seemed to be wandering into a maze; and, like a maze, Prosper Station unfolded its wonders to her.

In many ways, it did not belie its name. The corridors were vast and warm, decorated with hologram works of art, from images of waterfalls on the Fifth Planet, to a lonely house clinging to the mountain, lost in morning mist. Here and there, quatrains spoke of the wonders of coming home, of the sorrow of parting and the fall of the Old Empire...

In other ways...Linh had once been to the capital, and had seen the epitome of refinement there—the inlaid marble panels, brought all the way back from Old Earth, the exquisite calligraphy that breathed and seemed to move with a life of its own, like a coiled dragon hidden within text. For all its wealth, Prosper Station remained a small, isolated station at the back end of nowhere, on the edge of the Dai Viet Empire. The poems were quotations taken from old books, and not the vibrant, searing words traded in the literary clubs on First Planet; the paintings, too, were old, and looked like they hadn't been refreshed for a while; and the architecture of the corridors was a little too bulky, a little too clumsy, lacking the effortless flowing grace of more central habitats.

There was a faint music of zither in the background, which got stronger as they crossed room after room; and a faint smell, like the one after the rain. The walls flared out, and they were walking through carefully preserved gardens, with the smell of bamboo and phuong grass heavy in the air, a luxury that must have all cost a fortune in air and water and heat.

Linh felt a thread at the back of her mind: Fifth Ancestor Hoang, trying to push her into reading the poems which named each area, to admire the designers' culture, their clever allusions to the poets of the past. Fifth Ancestor, ever the poet, ever the lover of history. She pushed him back, gently, ignoring the suggestion. It wasn't time for cleverness or beauty; though Fifth Ancestor whispered in her mind that there was always time for beauty, that one who did not pause to admire beauty might as well be dead to the world.

At length, they reached a room almost hidden away amidst the greenery. The door slid open at a touch of the young man's fingers; he moved away to let Linh in.

Within, everything seemed almost bare, until she realised that the shimmer on the red walls was text. Word after word scrolled from top to bottom, almost too fast to read. Linh caught fragments about moonlight, and jade, and wild herds of trau cho soi over the plains; verse after verse, more clever allusions than her mind would ever hold, even with her mem-implants.

Beautiful.

A woman was waiting for her there, frozen in the uncertain land between youth and old age, too old to be patronised, too young to be respected. Behind her was a younger girl, waiting with her head bowed, though everything in her spoke of arrested flight. "Be welcome here, cousin." A brief burst of trance, and Linh was tracing the trees. Yes, they were indeed cousins, through her maternal grandmother, and the woman's marriage to Lê Nhu Anh, and...

The world wobbled and crumpled, as if it were a sheet of paper the spirits had punched through. There was a presence in the room; the text shimmered, the letters becoming subtly distorted, the red of the walls taking on an oily sheen, like fish sauce mixed with grease, and a wind too cold to be any draught. It was all she could do not to fall to her knees, her mind struggling to cope with it all...

She hadn't come unprepared, of course. She'd read all about the stations, all about the Minds that held and regulated them, all about stations like Prosper and its Honoured Ancestress, and the family that peopled its core. But the truth of a Mind's presence shattered the easy descriptions, the facile, clever similes written as glibly as inferior poems: it was its own self, the vast, dark presence that seemed to fold the air around itself, wrapped around the contraption in the centre of the room that might have been a throne, that might have been a tree with too many thorns; metal, twisting and buckling like a fish caught on land, its shifting reflections hurting her eyes...

"Welcome home, child," a voice said, filling her ears to bursting.

"Great-great-grandmother." She forced herself to get the words out, even as the trance went wild, seeking a pathway that would connect her to the Mind, ancestor after ancestor overlaid over the twisting texts. "I apologise for disturbing you."

A sound which might have been laughter. "Nonsense.

Whenever did my children ever disturb me? This is your house, and you're always welcome here."

Even the words were wrong, subtly off, evoking a burst of recognition from First Ancestor Thanh Thuy, vocabulary and phrases reminding Linh of old memorials, not used for many generations. She triggered her mem-implants, letting First Ancestor's mem-fragments flood her mind, picking out words as they surfaced. "Heaven and Earth have overturned for me. I seek refuge in the embrace of my family."

Another vast, ineffable sound: a chuckle or a sniff of anger? The pressure against her mind didn't seem unfriendly. "This was your great-grandfather's home. It's also yours, should you wish it. What is it that you seek refuge from?"

Linh hesitated a fraction of a second, as all six ancestors in her mind howled at her for daring to lie to a superior; and then said, each word as dry as sun-baked chillies on her tongue, "War has come to the Twenty-Third Planet, and to the province of Great Light. My tribunal burns in the riots, and lawless soldiers scour the streets with their war-kites, raping and pillaging as they go."

It was untrue. The news of the war had reached her only after her ship pulled itself out of the deep planes: pictures of her tribunal in flames, the litany of the dead, of the missing she couldn't trace. All because her first lieutenant Giap had tricked her into running, into abandoning her own people...

For a moment, a bare, agonising moment, a suspended

155

breath, she thought the Mind had caught her. She felt her pulse race in its wide-spectrum vision, caught the sheen of sweat on her brow, or ten thousand other ways she could have given herself away. But at length, the pressure retreated; and in the centre of the room, the core was inert again, and the only memory of the Mind's presence in the room was a faint whisper: "You have my blessing, child."

Linh bowed, very low, as low as she'd have bowed for the Emperor, letting a dozen heartbeats pass before she rose again.

The woman, Lê Thi Quyen, was waiting for her, as unmoving and as expressionless as propriety required. "Come, Cousin," she said. "We'll see you settled properly." But as she turned away from the core Linh caught the slight, impatient shake of her head, and knew the Mind might have believed her, but Quyen would be watching, and waiting, on the lookout to expose her lies.

She might be family, as the Mind had said. But she wasn't welcome on Prosper Station.

Available through all major retailers (ebook)
and Createspace (print)

ALIETTE DE BODARD

SERVANT OF THE
UNDERWORLD

BOOK 1 OF OBSIDIAN AND BLOOD

FOR NEWS ABOUT
JABBERWOCKY
BOOKS AND AUTHORS

Sign up for our newsletter*: http://eepurl.com/b84tDz
visit our website: awfulagent.com/ebooks
or follow us on twitter: @awfulagent

THANKS FOR READING!

*We will never sell or giveaway your email address, nor use
it for nefarious purposes. Newsletter sent out quarterly.